FROM THE NANCY DREW FILES

THE CASE: When a military academy turns into a murder scene, Nancy marches into action.

CONTACT: George's friend Charlie Burke never imagined his invitation would draw Nancy into a dangerous investigation.

SUSPECTS: Trevor Austin—The hothead believes women have no place at Stafford . . . and he may have taken matters into his own hands.

Tania Allens—A cadet pushed to the limit by Sergeant Grindle . . . and perhaps pushed over the edge.

Martin Royce—The academy's commander fears the truth . . . even to the point of covering up a murder.

COMPLICATION: Nancy's fallen under the spell of a certain captain . . . which could spell trouble in her relationship with Ned.

Books in The Nancy Drew Files® Series

Available from ARCHWAY Paperbacks

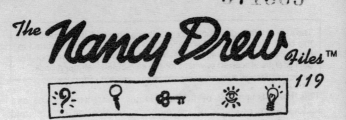

The *Nancy Drew* Files™

119

AGAINST
THE RULES

CAROLYN KEENE

AN ARCHWAY PAPERBACK
Published by POCKET BOOKS
New York London Toronto Sydney Tokyo Singapore

This book is a work of fiction. Names, characters, places and
incidents are products of the author's imagination or are used
fictitiously. Any resemblance to actual events or locales or persons,
living or dead, is entirely coincidental.

AN ARCHWAY PAPERBACK *Original*

An Archway Paperback published by
POCKET BOOKS, a division of Simon & Schuster Inc.
1230 Avenue of the Americas, New York, NY 10020

ISBN: 0-671-56877-9

First Archway Paperback printing February 1997

10 9 8 7 6 5 4 3 2 1

Printed in the U.S.A.

IL 6+

AGAINST
THE RULES

Chapter

One

I'D LOVE TO DATE a guy in uniform," Bess Marvin said dreamily. Her blond head rested comfortably against the seat of the car as the autumn landscape whipped by outside the window.

"Really, Bess?" her cousin George Fayne asked. "Because I know of this gorgeous guy. He's behind bars, but you can wri—"

"You know what I mean, George!" Bess cried. "Military guys are so . . . romantic."

"Don't worry, Bess." Nancy Drew laughed as she maneuvered the steering wheel for a sharp curve in the road. "This weekend you'll get your chance."

George and Nancy smiled. Bess's extreme interest in romance was a long-standing joke

1

between them. She was always falling in and out of love, and always on the lookout for her next boyfriend, who usually wasn't far away.

"Nancy's right, Bess," George added from the backseat. "And you'll have hundreds of guys to choose from. That is, after you meet the really nice guy that Charlie has picked out for you. He's got one for you, too, Nan," she added.

George's friend, Charlie Burke, had invited the three girls to spend the long weekend at Stafford Military Academy to celebrate its one hundredth anniversary. There would be a formal dance, a few parties, a military ceremony, and, most important, the chance to meet lots of cadets.

"Really nice guys are fine, George," Bess said. "But what I want to know is, *are they cute?*"

George laughed at her cousin.

"Well, George, are they?" Nancy asked.

"But, Nancy, you have Ned. I didn't think *you'd* be on the lookout for any handsome and charming cadets," George said with a grin.

"You're right. I'm certainly not looking for a new boyfriend. But I do want to enjoy myself," Nancy responded. "And I wouldn't mind being distracted for a weekend," she added mischievously.

Nancy and Ned Nickerson had been dating for years. Sometimes they drifted apart, but they always found their way back to each other. Ned supported Nancy in everything she did. Even when her detective work meant that she sometimes ended up in dangerous situations, he never tried to stand in her way. Nancy loved that about him.

"Earth to Nancy," George said. "Do you want to know about your date, or do you want to be surprised?"

Nancy looked at George through the rearview mirror. "I think you'd better tell Bess about her date first or she'll explode."

"Okay." George leaned closer to the front seats of Nancy's Mustang. "From what Charlie told me about Trevor Austin, he sounds perfect for you," she said to Bess. "He's a second lieutenant, one of the highest-ranking cadets. Charlie chose him because I told him you love parties. He says that Trevor's the best dancer at Stafford Academy."

"And the big formal is tonight, Bess," Nancy added.

"Terrific!" Bess was wide-eyed. She tilted her head to one side and gave George a grin. "But you still haven't told me if he's cute."

George wrinkled her nose. "Gee, Bess, I didn't tell Charles he had to pick good-looking dates for us." She laughed when she saw Bess's mouth drop open. "Relax! I've seen a picture of Trevor, and he's definitely good-looking. He has blond hair and a smile that would melt any girl's heart. He'll be *perfect* for you."

"My turn," Nancy said. "Even though my heart belongs to Ned."

"Wait until you hear this." George leaned closer. "Your escort is Captain Nicholas Dufont, the battalion commander. He's in charge of all the other cadets at the academy."

"Sounds good," Nancy said as she turned the car off the highway and onto a two-lane road shaded by maple trees.

"Is that all you're going to say?" Bess asked with amazement. "Aren't you the least bit curious about him?"

"Not really," Nancy said. "I'm just going to this thing to enjoy myself with my two best friends." She paused, then smiled broadly. "And hundreds of gorgeous cadets."

The three girls burst into laughter.

"Wow!" Nancy exclaimed as she slowed the car at the front gate of Stafford Military Academy. "This place is incredible!" Before them lay hundreds of rolling acres dotted with imposing redbrick buildings. In the distance, they could see people marching in perfect step.

She rolled down the window and showed their guest pass to a cadet inside the guardhouse. "Welcome to Stafford Academy," he said with a polite smile. "Drive straight through until you get to the main building. You can't

4

miss it—it's the one with the circular driveway. Pull your car up to the front door of the main building. The reception area is just inside the lobby. There, someone will check you in and direct you to the hotel."

"Thanks," Nancy said as the guard waved them through the gate. "George, where are the guys meeting us?"

"At the reception area," George answered.

A few minutes later, Nancy stopped the car in front of a large redbrick building with white columns. She handed the keys to a cadet who was waiting at the door and asked him to have their car and luggage taken to the on-campus hotel.

As soon as Nancy stepped onto the plush carpet of the lobby, she was embraced by the scent of freshly cut roses. "This place is spectacular," she said to her friends, looking up at the sweeping circular staircase and the crystal chandelier high above.

"George!" A tall red-haired cadet rushed to greet them.

"Hi, Charlie!" George called. Charlie approached eagerly, followed by two other cadets. One was of medium height and muscular, with blond hair. The other was taller, with dark hair, and was strikingly handsome. Nancy and the dark-haired young man looked at each other, and their eyes locked for a moment.

"It's great to see you, George," Charlie said, introducing her to his friends. "I'm Charlie Burke," he said, reaching out his hand to Nancy.

"Pleased to meet you," Nancy said, extending her hand.

"And, of course, you're Bess," Charlie said after a moment. "George gave me exact descriptions of you both. Ladies, I'd like you to meet Trevor Austin and Nicholas Dufont."

Nancy was pleased that the dark-haired cadet was to be her date for the weekend. She was so pleased, in fact, that she had a slight sensation of butterflies in her stomach. Now, *that* hardly ever happens, Nancy thought to herself.

"I thought we'd start the weekend with a tour of the place," Nicholas said, offering Nancy his arm.

"I'd like that," Nancy said, meeting his gaze. His eyes were an unusual blue-gray color. Nancy was impressed with his intelligent, intense expression. She had the feeling those eyes didn't miss much.

"So . . . you're the battalion commander," Nancy said as they strolled down a gravel path that led to the rest of the campus. "That sounds like a pretty big job."

Nicholas smiled a warm, genuine smile that lit up his entire face. "It is. It's also an honor," he said. "I work with the administration in planning everything from cadet disciplinary policies to day-to-day student activities. It's been a great experience."

Nancy heard the pride and sincerity in his voice. "It must be quite a challenge," she said.

"It can be," Nicholas replied. "The program here is really demanding, geared to prepare cadets to succeed in whatever they choose to do in life—whether or not it's a military career. Some cadets get thrown by the demands and may even think they can't cut it. I try to help them over the rough spots, or help them make the decision that the program just isn't right for them."

"Do they always agree with you?" Nancy asked.

Nicholas laughed. "It would sure be a lot easier if they did! But naturally, not everyone does. One of the toughest things I've ever had to do is to tell a cadet that he's just not meeting the requirements and that he has to leave. In most cases, though, it's the best thing."

Nancy was impressed by Nicholas's commitment. He projected maturity and strength without making a show of it. It was easy to imagine him rising through the ranks to become a leader.

"Here are some of our plebes now." Nicholas pointed to a line of young men and women running toward them single file on a jogging path. "The plebes are freshmen. We begin the weeding-out process from the very beginning. We really put the new cadets through their paces."

In striking contrast to the sweaty, weary-looking bunch of plebes, a young woman trotted on the grass that bordered the jogging trail. She showed no outward sign of effort. Even in the school's winter training outfit—dark sweatpants, a sweatshirt with the Stafford Military Academy logo, and a knitted cap—she looked as if she had just stepped out of a fashion magazine. Her clear skin glowed, and her auburn hair shone in the sun.

"Let's get it up to speed, Allens!" she barked at a straggler, a slight young woman with dark hair. The girl was panting harder than any of the other cadets and looked as if she was barely able to take another step. "No slacking off!" the young woman barked in the girl's ear. "Move it!"

"Who's the drill sergeant?" Nancy asked.

Nicholas shook his head. "That's Stephanie Grindle," he said. "She's a squad leader and one of the toughest cadets at the academy. Some people think she's a little too tough."

"Hey, Nick!" Trevor Austin called as he and Bess caught up to Nancy and Nicholas. "What chance do you think Tania Allens has of sticking it out? Off the record, I mean."

Nancy saw Nicholas hesitate. "Cadet Allens is having a rough time. I thought a tough squad leader like Stephanie would help her shape up, but I'm beginning to wonder if this was a wise course of action. She's already getting a lot of flak from the other female cadets." He turned to Nancy. "The female cadets can be tougher on one another than even the toughest squad leaders."

"Oh, come on, Nick," Trevor objected. "Almost every day it's boo-hoo-hoo. I can't believe she made it this far," he said with obvious disgust. "She should have been booted out a long time ago."

"Well, she *is* a cadet, Trevor," Nicholas said with an edge of annoyance in his voice, "and because of that, she deserves your respect."

There was a moment of uncomfortable silence. Nancy sensed that there was more going on than just a disagreement over Tania Allens's suitability for the academy, though she couldn't quite tell what it was.

"Understood," Trevor said, and the uncomfortable moment passed. "I guess I did get a little carried away," he added. "I'm proud of the place, that's all, and—"

An earsplitting shriek ripped through the air, cutting off Trevor's words.

In a moment, the foursome was racing in the

direction of the scream. A line of ashen-faced cadets were already there. "What seems to be the problem here?" Nicholas said as he made his way through the crowd. At the center of the group was Stephanie Grindle. Lying motionless on the ground was Tania Allens.

Chapter

Two

"ON YOUR FEET, Allens!" Stephanie ordered. Her face was a cold mask of disgust.

Tania Allens groaned. "I'm injured, ma'am." She tried to raise herself to a sitting position. Her face contracted in pain as she winced and reached for her ankle.

"Get up!" the squad leader barked again. "That's an order!"

Tania Allens cradled her head in her hands, and her shoulders began to shake with her sobbing. "I can't get up," she cried. "I just can't. I think I've sprained my ankle."

Stephanie shook her head impatiently. "Quit whining. We've all had enough of that from you."

"Come on, Tania. Don't pull this again,"

goaded a cadet with a round, freckled face and red hair.

"Quiet!" Stephanie snapped. She shot the redheaded cadet a withering look that made the plebe's face turn the same shade as her hair. "I'm in command of this unit, not you. Is that clear?" Stephanie said.

"Yes, Sergeant," the cadet replied.

Stephanie turned back to scrutinize her original target. "Five demerits, Allens!" she said harshly. "You're well on your way to racking up enough to get yourself on probation, and frankly, nothing would make me happier. Now, get back to the barracks!"

A choking sound came from Tania's throat. She struggled to her feet and stumbled as her foot gave way. Then she half-jogged, half-limped to catch up with her squad.

During the whole scene, Nancy noticed that several of the other cadets looked away, clearly embarrassed. A few, however, glared at Tania with open hostility.

That isn't discipline, Nancy thought, it's downright cruelty. She waited to see how Nicholas would handle the situation.

"Back into formation," Stephanie shouted to her squad. She turned around and seemed to realize for the first time that Nicholas and the others had heard her berating Tania. She looked a little flustered as she saluted the battalion commander.

Nicholas returned the salute and dropped his hand. "What just happened, Grindle?"

Stephanie stood at attention. "Cadet Allens failed to execute the hand-by-hand overhead for the fourth time and dropped to the ground, sir."

Nancy looked up and saw loops of rope laced in an overhead ladder through the trees. She recognized the maneuver, which involved jumping up and grasping each rung of rope to pull oneself over to the other side. It had to be a difficult task—the overhead loops extended for at least thirty feet.

"All of the other cadets have completed the maneuver successfully," Stephanie went on. "In addition, Cadet Allens constantly lags behind on training runs and has failed her room inspection on several occasions. She can't cut it, sir. I recommend she be placed on probation."

"Now isn't the time for recommendations like that, Sergeant," Nicholas said. "Write up a report, and bring it to my office tomorrow at eleven hundred hours. At that time, we will review your disciplinary tactics as well."

"Yes, sir." Sergeant Grindle blushed. Nancy thought she looked upset at Nicholas's criticism of her.

"Carry on, Sergeant," Nicholas said.

Stephanie's hand snapped into a salute. Nicholas returned the salute briefly and watched as Stephanie led her squad away.

"Ahem . . ." Charlie cleared his throat to signal that he and George were approaching.

Nicholas turned back to his guests. "I'm sorry about that," he said.

With a smile, he became the perfect host once more. "Let's go to the boathouse. There's a café there with the world's best cappuccino."

"Great idea," Nancy said.

Nicholas led the way to a long, white, wooden building that overlooked the water.

The boathouse café was a cozy room where several lively groups were sitting around rustic wooden tables. As soon as the waiter saw Nicholas and his friends, he hurried over.

"Cappuccinos all around, if that's all right with everyone," Nicholas said as they sat down at a table. Everyone agreed.

"Wait until you taste this cappuccino," Charlie said. "You'll think you're in Italy."

Moments later, the waiter returned with steaming cups brimming with frothy white milk and topped with cinnamon. Nancy wrapped her hands around her cup to warm them and took a sip. "This is fantastic," she said.

"Yeah, great," Trevor muttered. He tapped his spoon irritably on the table.

Charlie raised his eyebrows. "What's your problem?"

Trevor pushed his cup forward and frowned. "Nothing."

Charlie stared at him. "You're obviously angry about something."

Trevor let out his breath in an explosive burst. "It's Grindle!" he blurted out. "Her style of command is way out of line. She's tough at the expense of her squad. That's not leadership."

Nancy, Bess, and George exchanged glances. So far, this wasn't shaping up to be the fun weekend they had hoped for.

"Hold on, Trevor." Charlie leaned across the table toward him. "Other sergeants are just as tough on their squads. What's your beef with Stephanie?"

"She should have at least checked to see if Allens was really hurt," Trevor snapped.

"Okay," Charlie agreed. "But you've said plenty of times yourself that you don't think Tania Allens belongs here anyway. So what's really on your mind?"

"You know as well as I do what the problem is around here," Trevor said.

"Why don't you fill us all in?" Nicholas said.

"Female cadets!" Trevor spat out the words. "Women have no business in the military. They don't have the constitution."

"That's enough, Trevor!" Nicholas interrupted. He spoke quietly but with such authority that Trevor fell silent immediately. "Any cadet who meets the requirements is qualified to remain at the academy. Being female or male isn't the issue. Besides," he said, nodding toward Nancy, Bess, and George, "you're being rude to our guests."

"Sorry, ladies. I'd better cool off." Trevor pushed his chair back abruptly, stood up, and stalked out of the café.

"I'll go talk to him," Charlie said, beginning to get up.

Nicholas put a restraining hand on his arm. "Let him go. He'll be okay." He looked around the table. "I apologize, ladies. Trevor can be a little hotheaded sometimes."

Nicholas gave a good-natured smile, but Nancy could see the storm clouds that darkened his blue-gray eyes. She admired his graciousness and composure, and her interest in him increased.

"Let me tell you all something about Trevor." Nicholas touched Nancy's hand for a brief instant, a touch that surprised her by sending an electric tingle down the length of her arm.

"Trevor is still seething over a slap on the wrist he got from Stephanie. She caught him out after taps, and he ended up with fifteen hours of tours."

"Tours?" Bess asked.

"He had to march back and forth in full dress in the barracks yard for fifteen hours," Charlie answered.

"That seems a bit harsh," George said.

"But how could Stephanie discipline Trevor when he outranks her?" Nancy asked.

"That's what burns Trevor more than anything," Nicholas said. "Stephanie is on the Honor Board, a group of cadets able to vote on disciplinary matters. She persuaded the others to hand out the toughest punishment allowed for his offense, and Trevor found out about it.

"To make things worse," Nicholas went on, "I think Trevor still has a crush on Stephanie."

"I'll bet you're right," Charlie said. "Poor guy—punished in more ways than one!" He laughed.

Charlie had an infectious laugh that lightened the mood, and soon everyone at the table joined in. Only Bess looked glum, Nancy noticed.

"Tell us about the weekend, guys," Nancy said, hoping to cheer up her friend.

For the next half hour, Charlie and Nicholas talked about the formal planned for that evening, the jeans party, a special training demonstration, and some of the other weekend activities.

As the conversation continued, Nancy found she couldn't take her eyes off Nicholas. She had to admit to herself that she was definitely attracted to him—he was handsome and intelligent, and he exuded a confidence that she found irresistible.

By the time the guys dropped Nancy, Bess, and George at the hotel, Nancy was feeling a mixture of excitement and confusion. But the sight of Bess's troubled expression snapped her out of her own thoughts.

"You look positively down in the dumps, Bess." Nancy put her arm around her friend as they headed up the walk toward the hotel.

Bess bit her lip. "It's Trevor. George said he was perfect. I think he's a perfect jerk. His attitude about women is totally hostile. Where did Charlie find him, anyway—back in the Stone Age? I'm almost sorry we came here."

"Cheer up, Bess," Nancy said as they reached the front door. "Trevor is angry at Stephanie, and he seems to be taking it out on every woman he knows. By tonight he'll probably have cooled off. And remember, he *is* the best dancer at the academy."

Nancy was about to say something more when the sound of angry voices from the parking lot made her stop short. This was no ordinary argument. The two voices, one male and one female, were making quite a scene.

"You just don't understand how important it is for me to excel." The female voice was angry and bitter-sounding.

"You've gone too far this time, Stephanie," said a deep voice shaking with rage. "You want to get ahead, and you don't care who you hurt to do it. Well, you've hurt too many people, and this time I'm not going to be one of them. I won't let it happen."

"That's Stephanie arguing with someone," Nancy said. The two voices sounded so charged with fury that she was worried about where it might lead. Yet she wasn't sure if intervening at this point might make things worse. She exchanged worried glances with Bess and George.

"Don't be ridiculous," Stephanie said. "I'm only doing what I need to do. You're behaving like a spoiled brat, only thinking of yourself."

"It's about time I did," the masculine voice growled back. "Listen to me, Stephanie. This is the last time you'll get away with this. I'm not going to put up with it anymore."

"Oh, really?" Stephanie taunted. "Just what do you think you're going to do about it?"

There was a moment of silence as Nancy, Bess, and George held their breath.

"Stay away from me!" Stephanie shrieked. Now there was a trace of panic in her voice. "Don't!"

They heard Stephanie let out a scream, followed by the sound of breaking glass. Then there was silence.

Chapter

Three

BEFORE NANCY, Bess, and George could reach the parking lot, they heard a car door slam. They arrived as a dark blue sedan sped away with a squeal of tires. Stephanie stood watching it go. Nancy tried to get the license number, but the car was moving too quickly for her to catch anything.

"Are you all right?" Nancy asked breathlessly as she reached Stephanie's side.

"What do you mean?" Stephanie stared at Nancy as if nothing whatsoever were wrong.

"We thought we heard an argument, and things sounded pretty ugly," Nancy said, a hint of surprise in her voice. "When we heard breaking glass, we thought you might be in danger."

"Oh, *please.*" Stephanie waved her hand as if to dismiss the whole incident. "It was only a perfume bottle." She pointed to the shards of glass on the pavement in a pool of liquid. "Nice gift, huh?" Stephanie looked at Nancy, and her eyes narrowed. "Why all the questions?"

Nancy recognized the edge in her voice. "We were just concerned," she replied calmly.

"Well, thanks just the same. But I'd appreciate it if you'd mind your own business." Stephanie's voice was harsh as she turned on her heel and walked away.

"I think her uniform's on too tight," George muttered, looking after her.

"Yeah," Bess agreed. "Of all the ungrateful—"

"Oh, never mind," Nancy said. "She's just upset. I'm sure she's embarrassed that we heard the whole thing."

"Everyone's upset around here," Bess grumbled. "First Trevor, then Stephanie. Who's next? This is definitely not the fun weekend Charlie promised us."

"Come on," Nancy said, putting an arm around Bess's shoulder and steering her back toward the hotel. "You'll feel better after a shower and some rest."

A few hours later, rested and refreshed, the girls stood in their hotel room, clad in bathrobes. Clothing was strewn everywhere. Formal dresses lay across the cream-colored bedspreads and were draped over the backs of chairs. Open suitcases overflowed with jeans and blouses. Shoes were all over the carpet, and jewelry covered the bureau.

"Nancy, which do you like better," Bess asked, "the blue silk or the violet chiffon?" She held up two formal gowns.

Although the girls had decided what to wear to the formal dance while they were still at home, they had each brought an extra dress in case they changed their minds.

Nancy tilted her head to one side and considered Bess's possibilities. "They're both gorgeous, Bess. And both colors are good for you. I guess it all depends on which one you feel like wearing," she said.

Bess sighed. "I'll never be able to decide."

"It doesn't matter." Nancy laughed. "You'll look great in either dress."

"Well, what about the jewelry?" Bess asked. "What looks best on me?"

Nancy went to the dresser and picked up a dangling earring with sparkling blue stones and another made of a single purple stone. She held them both up to Bess's face and studied the effect critically. "I think the violet is more dramatic," she said.

"I was hoping you'd pick that one," Bess said happily. "I knew it was the right one all along."

Nancy and George exchanged their "she's

hopeless" smiles, then went back to concentrating on their own outfits.

"Could I borrow your gold bracelet, Nancy?" George asked.

"Sure, go ahead," Nancy said. "I think I've settled on this burgundy satin and the necklace with deep red stones." Nancy held the gown and necklace up for inspection.

"That's perfect!" George and Bess exclaimed at once.

Nancy stood before the mirror and studied her reflection.

The off-the-shoulder gown was flattering and sophisticated. It set off her reddish blond hair, which she had swept up into a French twist. Her necklace provided just the right finishing touch.

Nancy's eyes sparkled. Several times while she was getting dressed, she had imagined herself dancing with Nicholas. Each time she created the picture in her mind, her heart beat a little faster and her cheeks felt warm. She felt a twinge of guilt as she realized she had barely thought of Ned since she'd met Nicholas.

When the phone rang, all three girls jumped, then burst out laughing. George answered.

"We'll be down in a sec," she said, and hung up the phone. "They're downstairs waiting for us."

Nancy smoothed her dress, pulled a cape

around her shoulders, and picked up her evening bag. "Ready, ladies?" she asked, twirling around in front of the mirror one last time.

Downstairs, Charlie, Trevor, and Nicholas stood near the front of the lobby. As the three girls approached, they removed their hats.

Nancy's and Nicholas's eyes met and held. The electricity between them fairly crackled in the air.

Nancy thought Nicholas looked irresistible in his full-dress uniform. A blue-gray sash stretched across his chest, and his hat was decorated with gold braid. There were also gold braid epaulets on his shoulders and four stripes on his sleeve, which showed the rank of captain.

"You look beautiful, Nancy," Nicholas said as he approached.

She felt a delicious shiver as she returned his gaze. "Thank you," she whispered. Her heart was beating so hard she could feel it pounding against her chest.

"My car is outside," Nicholas said, taking Nancy's arm. "The Grand Ballroom is on the other side of the campus, near the boathouse. I figured you'd done enough walking for one day and would prefer to ride."

"You're right." Nancy smiled, enjoying the warmth of his touch.

She was glad she and Nicholas would be

riding in his car by themselves. She had to admit, that she wanted to be alone with him.

During the ride to the Grand Ballroom, the two said very little. The attraction between them was so strong it left Nancy speechless.

"The campus looks beautiful at night," Nancy murmured finally.

Nicholas nodded. "Sometimes I stand outside my dorm on nights like this and stare at the stars," he said. "It's magical."

They fell silent again until Nicholas stopped the car in front of an ivy-covered building that glowed with light. "Here we are," he said. He got out of the car and went around to open the door for Nancy, then handed the keys to a valet.

Nancy was completely unprepared for what happened when they entered the Grand Ballroom. There were murmurs throughout the crowd as all eyes turned toward the battalion commander and his date. Then a hush fell over the room.

A cadet who was standing by the door announced their arrival. "Captain Nicholas Dufont and Ms. Nancy Drew."

All the cadets in the room stood at attention and saluted their commanding officer. Nicholas returned the salute and led Nancy to the center of the dance floor.

Immediately, the band began to play a waltz, signaling that the dance had officially begun.

Nicholas took Nancy in his arms, and they began to move effortlessly to the music. As the rest of the academy and guests looked on, Nicholas led Nancy around the dance floor. Around and around they went, gazing into each other's eyes. For a moment, Nancy forgot the many faces that surrounded them as they danced.

When the song ended, the room burst into applause. Nicholas bowed to Nancy, then reached for her hand and kissed it lightly.

"Gosh," Nancy breathed. "That's quite an opening dance."

Nicholas smiled. "I'm glad you were my partner," he said. "I don't usually like being the center of attention. Luckily, all eyes were on you."

Before long, the ballroom dance numbers gave way to the beat of rock music. A cheer went up as the dance floor became one happy throng. The music was so loud that Nancy and Nicholas didn't try to talk for a while. Instead, they lost themselves to the pulsing beat.

Finally, Nicholas put his hands together in a T shape to signal time out. "Let's take a break," he said to Nancy, his lips so close they brushed her ear.

Nancy nodded, and he led her from the dance floor to a long table filled with hors d'oeuvres.

Behind it, waiters poured beverages into chilled glasses.

"It's a good thing you suggested we take a break. I didn't realize how thirsty I was," Nancy said, taking a sip of sparkling water. She felt breathless but knew it was more from Nicholas's nearness than from the dancing.

Nicholas touched her shoulder gently. "Look over there," he said. "They're still dancing."

Nancy followed the direction of his gaze and saw George and Charlie, their bodies moving and swaying in time to the music. They were the most dynamic couple on the floor.

"They look great out there," Nancy said, taking another sip of water. "George is an athlete through and through.

"Speaking of athletes," Nancy continued, "where is Stephanie Grindle? I'd say she's about the only one who might be able to keep up with George on the dance floor."

Nicholas scanned the ballroom. "I don't see her," he said after a moment. Then he shook his head. "It's just like Stephanie to stay away from the dance. She's probably getting in extra practice for tomorrow's training maneuvers."

He knitted his brow. "I admire her determination, but everyone's got to learn to balance work and play."

Nancy was about to tell Nicholas about the

fight she, Bess, and George had overheard between Stephanie and the guy in the parking lot,
when a small commotion in the corner caught
her attention.

Bess and Trevor were not dancing—in fact, it
was clear to Nancy they were having a disagreement. Trevor was gesturing wildly as he spoke,
while Bess stood stiffly with her arms folded
over her chest.

Then it appeared that Trevor said something
that made Bess decide she'd had enough. With
a toss of her hair, she stormed away from him.

"Excuse me," Nancy said to Nicholas. She
hurried after Bess and caught up with her just
as she was about to leave the ballroom.

"Bess, what happened?" she said with concern in her voice.

Bess stamped her foot in frustration. "That
guy is getting on my nerves. I think I'll just go
back to the hotel."

Nancy glanced back to the spot where Trevor
had been standing. "I think he's leaving. Why
don't you stay? There are lots of other guys here
to dance with."

A smile flickered on Bess's lips. "You have a
point there."

No sooner were the words out of her mouth
than a tall cadet with blue eyes and a dazzling
smile appeared at her side. "Pardon me, miss.
Would you like to dance?" he asked.

"Sure." Bess nodded. "See you later, Nancy," she said brightly as she headed for the dance floor.

"I guess Bess and Trevor weren't meant for each other," Nicholas said as Nancy returned to his side. "I'm sorry."

"Take a look out there," Nancy said, nodding to the dance floor, where Bess and her new cadet friend were swaying to the music. "When it comes to men, Bess bounces back faster than anyone I know." She and Nicholas both laughed.

"Let's go for a walk outside, Nancy. We can admire the moonlight some more."

Nancy blushed and accepted the arm Nicholas offered with a smile. Wordlessly, they swept out of the ballroom, then retrieved their coats on their way out of the building. Nicholas led the way down a walkway between the trees until the loud music faded into the background.

They stopped at a spot that looked out over a valley lit by the bright moon and starry sky. "You're a wonderful dancer, Miss Drew." Nicholas placed his arm around Nancy as if to warm her.

"You're not so bad yourself, Captain Dufont." Nancy spoke out toward the valley. She knew if she turned to face him, she was going to kiss him. She'd never met anyone with whom she had shared such an immediate attraction.

Nicholas turned Nancy to face him. Then, tilting her chin upward, he leaned down and brushed her lips lightly with his own. She looked into his eyes, hoping he would kiss her again. A thought of Ned flashed across her mind, but she couldn't help leaning toward Nicholas, losing herself in the kiss until she felt as if she were floating.

Nancy stepped back to look at Nicholas and felt as if she were drowning in the blue-gray pools of his eyes. Then she put her cheek against his chest and closed her eyes, listening to the beating of his heart.

I'm not going to think about anything but what's happening right here, right now, she told herself.

Nancy opened her eyes and looked into the darkness. She blinked as something on the ground between the trees caught her eye. Her instinct told her something was wrong.

"I see something over there, Nicholas," she said, a shiver of fear running through her. "Something tells me we'd better find out what it is."

Together, Nancy and Nicholas hurried to get a look at what she had seen. Nancy drew in her breath sharply. Lying on the ground was

Stephanie Grindle, pale and still in the moon-light.

Nancy knelt down to feel Stephanie's pulse, then looked up at Nicholas with horror in her eyes.

"Now we know why Stephanie wasn't at the dance," Nancy said grimly. "She's dead."

Chapter

Four

POLICE SIRENS cut through the still night. The beams from the patrol cars' headlights brightened the area around Stephanie's body with a harsh white light. Every so often the crackle of a police radio scratched through the night air while officers strung yellow crime scene tape around the area.

A crowd gathered, growing larger as word of Stephanie's death spread. The police officers barked warnings for everyone to stay back.

Nancy shivered as she watched from behind the yellow tape. Nicholas had gone to notify the academy commander, and he hadn't yet returned. A few feet away, a police photographer snapped pictures of Stephanie's body. A uniformed officer was jotting down notes.

Nancy had studied the scene as she waited for

the police to arrive. What she had seen was disturbing.

A tall, heavyset man with gray hair cut through the crowd. In spite of the chill in the air, he was in his shirtsleeves. Behind him walked a taller, thinner man. Nancy recognized him as Academy Commander Martin Royce, whom Nicholas had pointed out at the ball.

He must be in charge of the case, Nancy thought as she observed the large man move with authority around the crime scene. She hoped she'd get a chance to speak with him.

After a few minutes, the heavyset man motioned to the photographer to stop taking pictures. Then he faced the crowd with his hands above his head to call for silence.

"May I have your attention, please?" he said. "I'm Detective Hugh Denman from police headquarters. I know you all must be upset about what just happened here. I assure you that a thorough investigation will be conducted. At the moment, we have every reason to believe that the death was accidental. This girl appears to have been practicing on the obstacle course tonight, and while running on the gravel path in the dark, she probably stumbled and hit her head."

A murmur raced through the crowd. The detective held up his hands for silence again. "Quiet, everybody! Quiet! Until a thorough investigation is conducted, there will be no further information. I'm going to ask everyone to clear the area now. Thank you."

The buzz of voices began again. The officers waved people away, and gradually the crowd dispersed in groups of two and three, talking among themselves.

Nancy stood her ground. She was surprised that the detective had been so quick to tell everyone that the death was accidental. She wondered if he had said it only to keep everyone calm.

She watched as the detective knelt down to study the body. Then he got to his feet and walked around the body, looking at the ground. He took a pad out of his pocket and scribbled something on it.

"Let's get a stretcher over here," he barked, waving to some attendants standing by an ambulance.

Nancy watched the scene with barely concealed frustration. Detective Denman had hardly examined the body before signaling for it to be removed. Her heart hammered. Something wrong was going on—very wrong. She could feel it.

She assumed the detective was going to have the body examined by forensic experts. But she knew that many things could be determined first from studying the body where it was found. He's disturbing the crime scene, Nancy thought.

She noticed Detective Denman say something to Commander Royce. He threw back his head and laughed, as if the two of them were sharing a private joke.

Nancy felt another stab of uneasiness. This man doesn't look the least bit concerned with conducting a thorough investigation, she thought as she watched. And how could he be laughing with a dead girl lying not three feet away from him on the ground?

As attendants placed the body on a stretcher and carried it to the ambulance, Nancy hurried to catch up with the detective, who was walking away with Commander Royce.

"Detective Denman," she called. "I wonder if I could speak with you." The detective appeared not to have heard Nancy. He and Commander Royce were walking briskly, deep in conversation. Nancy quickened her pace to catch up to them.

As Nancy neared the two men, she heard the detective's words as he spoke to the commander. "Don't worry, Martin. We'll have this thing wrapped up in no time. It's an accident, pure and simple."

"Excuse me, Detective Denman," Nancy said

breathlessly. "I'm Nancy Drew. My friend and I discovered the body. I thought you might want to ask me some questions."

Detective Denman stopped and turned to face Nancy. "No, dear, that won't be necessary," he said in a condescending tone. "Why don't you run along back to your dorm?" he added, as if he were speaking to a child.

The detective's tone stung Nancy like a slap in the face.

"I'm not sure you understand, Detective," Nancy said in a chilly tone. "I know I could be of help to you. My friend and I discovered Stephanie Grindle's body."

"The young lady's escort is Nicholas Dufont," the commander volunteered.

Detective Denman turned to Nancy and smiled. "We've already questioned your young man. He gave us all the facts. Now we have everything we need." His tone was dismissive, as if he were signaling no further conversation.

Nancy took a sharp breath. The way Denman was acting went against everything she knew about being a detective. He was blatantly disregarding the criminal investigation process—he seemed barely interested in gathering evidence.

"I believe I can tell you some things you might need to know." Nancy spoke in a no-nonsense voice. "I've had quite a bit of experience doing detective work myself."

Detective Denman faced Nancy squarely, his features puckered with annoyance.

"We appreciate your offer to help, Miss Drew," Commander Royce broke in. "But you needn't concern yourself with this investigation. Everything is under control."

Nancy's eyes narrowed as she watched the two men walk away.

The crowd was thinning rapidly, with police urging stragglers to move on. Nancy saw an officer heading toward her, so she started walking. Then she spotted Tania Allens up ahead, walking slowly and limping slightly.

"Tania—wait!" she called.

The plebe looked better than when Nancy had seen her that afternoon, but her eyes were red from crying. She brushed away a tear as Nancy approached. "What is it?" she asked in a choked voice.

"Hello, Tania. I'm Nancy Drew." She extended her hand.

Tania shook it weakly. "You're the detective," she said.

"How did you know that?" Nancy asked with surprise.

Tania shrugged and attempted a smile. "I heard Charlie talking about you with Captain Dufont and Trevor Austin," she said. "He sounded pretty excited about you and your friends coming up for the weekend."

Nancy smiled. "I'd like to ask you some questions about Stephanie Grindle," she said. "I know she was your squad leader."

"Sure, but I don't know how I could help you," Tania began, crying fresh tears. "I can't believe she's dead." She sobbed.

Nancy put a hand on Tania's shoulder. "I see you're very upset," she said. "Maybe we could talk first thing in the morning?"

Tania sighed wearily. "I guess so. I'll give you my room number."

Tania pulled a pencil and a small pad of paper out of her pocket and scribbled down the information. Then she tore off the piece of paper and handed it to Nancy. "You can come see me anytime. If I can help you, I will." She looked at Nancy with red eyes. "I really looked up to Stephanie."

Nancy thanked Tania and watched her walk away. Is it possible that Tania could admire someone who was so cruel to her? she wondered, remembering the scene on the obstacle course.

"Hey, Nancy! There you are! We've been looking for you."

Nancy looked around and saw Bess and George hurrying toward her. Charlie and Nicholas were with them.

Nicholas took her hands in his. "I'm sorry I've been so long. I had to find Commander

Royce at the dance, and then we went to his office to phone the police," he said. "Then the detective showed up, and I had to speak with him."

"What exactly did he want to know?" Nancy asked quickly.

Nicholas frowned. "Actually, he didn't ask all that many questions. Mostly he wanted to know if Stephanie spent much time alone. And he wanted to know if she went out running by herself a lot."

"What else?"

"Well, I told him that Stephanie was pretty tough on her squad."

"Did Detective Denman have anything to say about that?" Nancy asked.

"He took down the names of the members of the squad and said he'd contact them."

Well, well, Nancy thought to herself. The detective seems to know *something* about police procedure.

"Uh-oh," Bess said. "Here comes trouble— and its name is Trevor."

Trevor walked over to the group, his chin thrust out angrily. "I saw you talking to Tania Allens, Nancy," he said. "I heard you say you wanted to ask her some questions about Stephanie."

Nancy nodded. She could see that Trevor was seething with rage. Why could he possibly be so upset? she thought. He didn't even like Stephanie.

"You have no business meddling in an internal investigation," Trevor said with his face close to Nancy's. "You should mind your own business."

"Enough, Trevor!" Nicholas's voice sliced through the air.

"Why are you defending her?" Trevor raged. "You should back up your men!"

Nicholas's face wore a stunned expression, but he spoke with authority. "Trevor, you are totally out of line here. You are dismissed. Get back to your room immediately!"

The second lieutenant glared at Nicholas. His jaw was clenched.

Nicholas stared back, his gaze unwavering.

Then Trevor grunted and turned toward his dorm. He had gone only a few paces when he whirled around. For a moment he stood perfectly still, as if trying to decide what to do. Then he took off at a run. Nancy could see the pure anger in his eyes as he came toward them. With a bloodcurdling cry, Trevor lunged forward and hurled himself at Nicholas.

Chapter

Five

TREVOR'S FACE was twisted in an ugly mask of rage as his hands reached for Nicholas's throat. For Nancy, time seemed to stand still as Trevor's body arced through the air, closer and closer to Nicholas.

With lightning reflexes, Nicholas calmly took three quick steps backward. Trevor fell short of his mark and landed in the dirt, grunting as the wind was knocked out of him.

Nicholas stood watching Trevor but made no move to help him. After a moment Charlie helped Trevor to his feet. Trevor brushed himself off without looking at anyone. A gash was visible on his chin, and the front of his jacket was torn and dirty. His shoulders slumped dejectedly.

Nancy thought that the Trevor standing before her seemed a different person from the Trevor she had seen just a moment ago. It was as if a wild animal had possessed him and then suddenly left his body.

Nicholas stood clenching and unclenching his fists, his jaw set in a stony line.

"Get back to your room," Nicholas said quietly, but so coldly that it chilled Nancy's blood.

"I-I'm sorry. I don't know what came over me," Trevor stammered. Then he walked away, breaking into a run after a few yards.

Charlie stared after him. "Trevor's going through a tough time. You know how demanding his father is . . . well, he's turning up the heat. He wants Trevor to get even better grades and more awards—and no demerits at all. Trevor thinks nothing he does is good enough. It's got him wound up like a coiled spring."

"Well, he'd better unwind," Nicholas said through clenched teeth. "That attack was the last thing I needed tonight—and it just may go on his record."

He turned to Nancy. She could feel the tension radiating from him like heat. "He insulted you, and I'm sorry." His voice was still icy.

"It's over," Nancy said. "Trevor lost his head. I understand."

Nicholas took a deep breath. Then another.

When he spoke again, some warmth had returned to his voice, and he no longer seemed to be fighting for control. "Would you like me to take you back to the hotel?"

Suddenly Nancy felt very tired. "Yes, I would, thank you. It's been a long evening."

Sensing that Nancy might want to be alone with Nicholas, Bess turned to Charlie and George. "How about we head to the café before turning in? I could use a calming cup of tea," she said as she hurried them down the path.

Nancy took Nicholas's arm, and together they walked back to his car. On the way to the hotel, Nancy avoided mentioning her misgivings about Detective Denman's investigation. She didn't want to upset Nicholas any further.

She was surprised when Nicholas brought up the subject. "There's something bothering me about Detective Denman," he remarked. His voice was cool and analytical. "I'm no police professional, but his investigation seemed a little sloppy. What did you think?"

Nancy looked at his strong, handsome profile, silhouetted against the moonlight. I was right, she thought with admiration. Those eyes of yours don't miss very much.

"I have to agree with you, Nicholas," Nancy replied. "The whole thing felt wrong. I thought the detective was trying to keep the cadets calm, but when he didn't collect any evidence . . ." She let her voice trail off while her mind continued to puzzle over what had happened.

"Well, I'm going to look into it," Nicholas said.

Nancy didn't say anything. Her mind raced with ideas of her own, but she decided to keep them to herself for now. She knew Nicholas wouldn't be as hardheaded as Trevor, but she wasn't sure what his reaction would be to her plan to investigate on her own.

When they reached the hotel, Nancy and Nicholas said goodbye without any words, just a brief embrace.

Nancy went upstairs, tumbled into bed, and was fast asleep when Bess and George returned an hour later.

On Saturday morning, Nancy awoke when the first rays of sun streamed through the window. She sat up and stretched, wide awake and completely refreshed.

For a moment, only the romance of the night before occupied her thoughts. Then, at the sight of the muddy hem of her gown, the rest of the evening came flooding back, and she leaped out of bed.

Minutes later she had washed her face, brushed her teeth, and dressed in sneakers and sweats. After whispering "Good morning" to

Bess and George, who were just stirring, she took the elevator to the lobby and did some quick stretches just outside the door. Then she was off for a morning jog—to the crime scene.

As she ran, she became more and more certain that Stephanie's death was not an accident.

Nancy wished that she could have examined the scene more closely. Experience had taught her that it was best to look for clues as soon as possible, before any of the evidence had been disturbed. But she'd had only a few minutes alone with the body before the police arrived, and without a flashlight she hadn't been able to see much.

Soon Nancy hit her stride, a comfortable jog that let her cover ground quickly without becoming tired. The majestic scenery around her filled her eyes.

In the distance, she could see the sprawling white wooden boathouse beside the lake. The water sparkled in the sunlight.

Nancy's feet made crunching sounds as she ran through some leaves and onto the gravel path. Thoughts of her evening with Nicholas crowded her head.

A delicious shiver shot through her body as she recalled how it had felt when Nicholas had taken her in his arms to kiss her. Soon her heart was racing, and it wasn't from running.

Get a grip, a voice inside her head whispered. You're acting like you're in junior high. And what about Ned?

Her stomach twisted into a knot as the image of Ned's face appeared in her mind's eye, the way he looked when he told her that he loved her.

Nancy felt a wave of sadness wash over her. Her feelings for Ned were so strong, so real, and yet she was shocked to realize how easily Nicholas had entered her heart.

Discipline was the only thing that enabled Nancy to push the troubling thoughts from her mind. She forced herself to focus on the case, and by the time she was rounding the corner to the spot where Stephanie's body had been found, her mind was clear and sharp.

Nancy stopped just short of the yellow crime scene tape that cordoned off the area. Then she walked briskly back and forth to slow her breathing and cool down.

When she was ready to go to work, Nancy stepped cautiously under the yellow tape and stood still for a moment, trying to visualize everything she had seen the night before.

Stephanie's right leg had been twisted at an unnatural angle, and her arms were above her head, as if she had flung them out to break her fall—or to protect herself from an attacker, Nancy thought. She had noticed smudges of dirt on Stephanie's face, and her clothing had been slightly torn and dirty.

Nancy squeezed her eyes shut, reconstructing the scene. What was she leaving out of the picture?

Leaves! Nancy snapped her fingers. Stephanie's hair had been full of leaves.

Nancy began to piece together a possible scenario, guided by her instincts. The morning before, Stephanie had looked cool and exceptionally neat as she jogged along the obstacle course, in contrast to the weary, disheveled-looking plebes. It wasn't likely that Stephanie had torn and soiled her clothing going over a course she did easily almost every day.

Nancy began walking, her eyes searching the area.

After she had covered every inch of ground within the crime scene, Nancy slipped back under the yellow tape and began walking toward the obstacle course.

She had gone nearly a quarter of a mile before she found what she was looking for: bushes that had clearly been disturbed—bushes with leaves like the ones she had seen in Stephanie's hair. There were no leaves like that anywhere near the spot where the body had been found.

Nancy felt a surge of satisfaction as her suspicion was confirmed: Stephanie must have been in a fight of some kind. In fact, it was clear that Stephanie had struggled while moving over a distance before she died. But that was only a small piece of the puzzle. Whom had she been fighting *with* was the next question.

Nancy searched the ground for other clues as she headed back to the crime scene while her mind ticked off possibilities.

Who would want to kill Stephanie? That was a tough one, Nancy thought. Judging from what she had already witnessed, there were plenty of possibilities.

Trevor was one possibility. He was angry with Stephanie because of the way she had treated him, and he resented her position of authority at the academy. He had lost his temper twice in one day and had displayed a tendency to fly off the handle. Yes, he's a good possibility, Nancy thought grimly.

Tania Allens was another suspect. Even though she had seemed genuinely distressed about Stephanie's death, Nancy had too much experience to cross anyone off her list for being upset.

Then there was the guy Nancy, Bess, and George had overheard Stephanie fighting with in the parking lot. The only thing Nancy knew about him was that he wasn't a cadet. She made a mental note to ask Tania if she knew anything about him when she questioned her.

A loud rustling of leaves made Nancy jump. Her eyes darted around wildly, searching for what had caused the noise.

A brownish gray squirrel skittered through a pile of leaves and crossed her path, then zipped up a tree.

Nancy touched her hand to her chest and let out a deep breath, then laughed to release some tension. I can't believe the great Nancy Drew panicked over a squirrel, she thought with a chuckle.

Nancy continued to search the ground, hoping to find anything that seemed out of the ordinary. Even the tiniest clue would help.

Then, out of the corner of her eye, Nancy spotted a bit of blue in the pile of brown and gold leaves the squirrel had run through.

Crouching down, Nancy pushed the leaves aside and picked up a blue knit cap. She had seen the plebes wearing hats like it when they'd jogged by the day before.

Well, it's a clue, Nancy thought. But I bet all the cadets wear this when they do training maneuvers.

It could even be Stephanie's, she thought, turning the cap inside out to look for a name tag. Just then Nancy felt something strike the back of her head sharply. Before she could cry out, she fell to the ground, pain exploding behind her eyes. Then everything went dark.

Chapter

Six

NANCY WANTED more than anything to sleep but used all of her willpower to force her eyes open.

She pressed her hands against the cold ground and carefully raised herself to a sitting position. Her fingers gently searched the back of her head until she found a lump that felt as if it was the size of an egg.

How long have I been lying here? she thought groggily. It felt as if hours had passed, but a quick check of her watch revealed that not more than ten minutes had gone by.

Nancy took several long, deep breaths. Gradually, her head began to clear, and she remembered that she had just found the cap. Her gaze darted back and forth, searching the ground around her.

No cap. She wasn't surprised. Someone thought it was important to keep it out of her hands—and worth the trouble to trail her and knock her out, she surmised.

Nancy gritted her teeth and got to her feet. A throbbing pain shot through her leg, and her head was spinning. Somehow, she'd have to get back to the main campus.

She had gone only a few steps when she spotted a car with Stafford Military Academy painted on its side pulling out of the parking lot of the Grand Ballroom.

"Hey!" Nancy stumbled toward the car with arms waving. "Wait up!"

The driver, a brown-haired cadet, pulled to a stop and peered out the window. "Well, hey there! Remember me—Steve Monroe?"

The moment he smiled, Nancy recognized the cadet who had asked Bess to dance the night before. "Sure." She managed to return the smile.

"Hop in," Steve said, leaning across the front seat to open the passenger door.

"You don't know what a lifesaver you are," Nancy said as she slid into the front seat.

"Are you okay?" Steve asked. "What happened?"

Nancy looked down and saw that her sweatshirt was muddy and her pants were torn. "I was out jogging, and I slipped on some wet leaves. I can imagine what I look like."

Steve shook his head. "You ought to go out with a buddy. It can be pretty deserted early in the morning, even on a big weekend like this. Especially after what happened last night, you want to be extremely careful."

"I guess you're right," Nancy said. "Listen," she added quickly, "could you drop me off at the hotel?"

"I'd be glad to," Steve said. He eased the car out onto the road. "Nancy, did Bess say anything about me?" he asked eagerly.

Nancy looked at the cadet and smiled. Although he had tried to ask the question lightly, she could tell how important the answer was.

"Sorry, Steve. I was asleep when Bess came in last night, and she was still asleep when I went out this morning," she answered.

"Oh." Steve drove on in silence until they reached the hotel. "Well, take care of yourself. And tell Bess I said hi, okay?" he asked as he pulled up to the curb.

"Definitely," Nancy said. She hopped out of the car and thanked him for the ride.

The poor guy has been "Bessed," she thought with a smile.

When Nancy reached her room, she saw that Bess and George had left a note telling her they had gone to breakfast. After Nancy showered and changed her clothes, she hurried across the campus to meet them at the main dining room. Her head was no longer throbbing quite so intensely.

Nicholas rose to his feet as Nancy neared his table. His eyes held a questioning look. "I was beginning to think you weren't going to show."

Nancy's heart skipped a beat as soon as she saw his face. "I'll explain as soon as I have something to eat," she said, sitting down. Her eyes searched the dining room. "Have you seen my friends?"

"Charlie took George out for a hike," he said. "Bess is holding court over there," he added with a chuckle.

Nancy spotted Bess sitting at a table surrounded by cadets and laughed. "She's going to break a lot of hearts this weekend."

"I think you're right." Nicholas grinned and looked at Nancy. "I hope *you* don't break any hearts around here." He took her hand and lowered his eyes.

Nancy was at a loss for words. She wanted to tell him about Ned, but she didn't want to break the spell.

"Let's eat." Nancy surveyed the plates piled high with food that covered the table. She decided she'd know what to do after a good meal. "I'm hungry, Nick, but not *that* hungry!"

Nicholas laughed shyly. "They were closing

the buffet. I didn't know what you liked, so I got a little bit of everything."

Nancy hadn't realized just how hungry she was. When she had finished some scrambled eggs, bacon, and toast, she pushed her plate away and folded her napkin in front of her.

"Okay," Nancy said seriously. "I have a lot to tell you." She leaned across the table and spoke in low tones. "I don't think Stephanie's death was an accident, and, like you, I plan to do some investigating." She paused. When Nicholas didn't protest her involvement, Nancy continued.

"This morning I jogged out to where we found Stephanie's body. I searched the area and found one of those knit hats you all wear when you're training outside. It must have been an important clue," Nancy went on, "because someone sneaked up behind me and knocked me out. When I came to, the cap was gone."

"Nancy!" Nicholas's eyes were full of concern. "You should have a doctor check you out."

"I'm all right," Nancy said. "Really."

Nicholas shook his head. "You're going to pay a visit to the infirmary just to make sure," he said firmly.

After a moment Nancy nodded. "Okay, I'll go. Right now, though, I want to talk about the investigation."

She reached into her bag and pulled out a pen

and a small notebook. "So far I can think of three people with motives for killing Stephanie: Tania Allens, a guy I heard her fighting with in the parking lot . . . and Trevor."

Shock registered on Nicholas's face. "You really think either Tania or Trevor is capable of murder?" He shook his head.

"We have to face the fact that it's a possibility, Nick," Nancy said quietly. "Do you have any idea whom Stephanie might have been arguing with yesterday?"

Nicholas shrugged. "I guess it could have been her boyfriend. I had heard that she's been seeing someone who's not a cadet, so I don't know his name or even what he looks like. Stephanie and I never discussed personal things."

Nicholas leaned back in his chair. "I hate to say it, Nancy, but I'm sure there are a lot of cadets who didn't like Stephanie. She was a good cadet, but she definitely wasn't here to make friends."

Nancy tapped her pen on the table. "That doesn't make things any easier. I think having a look at some records might help narrow down the list. I'd like to find out which cadets she gave the most demerits to or filed bad reports against, things like that. Will you help me?"

Nicholas sat upright in his chair. "You're talking about looking at confidential files. I can't, Nancy. I'm the top-ranking cadet on campus. Doing something like that would break the Stafford code."

Nancy touched Nicholas's hand. "I understand, Nicholas. I really do. But a possible murder is a lot more serious than looking at some student files. Besides, we won't get any help from Commander Royce. Don't you want to get to the bottom of this?"

Nancy looked steadily into Nicholas's eyes. His lips were set in a grim line. "All right," he said after a moment. "I'll help you."

"I need the computer to look at the files," Nancy said firmly.

Nicholas shook his head. "Too risky. Those files are confidential, of course, but the computer room is very open, and people are always coming and going. There is a records room where written reports are kept. I think I can get you in there. Still . . ."

"What?"

"You'd be a lot less conspicuous if you were in uniform. Anyone seen in civilian clothing in the records area would stand out." Nicholas crossed his arms over his chest. "And I haven't the slightest idea how to get you a cadet uniform."

A wide smile spread over Nancy's face. "I can take care of that," she said. "Can you meet me at the hotel in an hour and a half?"

Nicholas nodded. "I probably ought to have my head examined, but I'll do it."

Nancy stood up. "I'm the one whose head is going to be examined, remember? Walk me over to the infirmary, will you?"

At the infirmary, Nancy told the doctor she'd hit her head in a jogging accident. Dr. Lee, a crisp, no-nonsense man, examined her and gave her a clean bill of health. "Be careful, young lady," he said.

Good idea, Nancy said to herself as she was heading across the campus. She looked up and saw Tania Allens and hurried to catch up with her.

"Tania, do you have a few minutes?" she asked.

Tania gave her a friendly smile. She looked very different from the troubled girl of the night before. "Sure. We can go back to my room and talk if you want."

Nancy started to have second thoughts about Tania as a suspect. If she had resented Stephanie, she was doing a great job of hiding it.

"I really admired Sergeant Grindle," Tania was saying as she unlocked the door to her room. Nancy followed her inside. "She was a tough cadet. She could handle anything."

"Are all of the cadets' rooms alike?" Nancy asked as she followed Tania inside.

"No. The plebes' rooms are smaller."

Nancy eyed the single bed made up with a plain blue bedspread and the chest of drawers beside it. On the other facing wall was a small desk, a chair, and a bookcase filled with textbooks, several boxes of stationery, and spiral notebooks in various sizes.

"It looks like you just moved in. You don't have any pictures on the walls or anything," Nancy observed.

Tania twirled a piece of hair between her fingers. "Plebes aren't allowed," she said. "They only let you have stuff on the walls after your first year." She plunked herself down on the bed. "Have a seat."

Nancy sat down in the desk chair. She decided to get right to the point. "Tania, I have to ask you a few tough questions," she said gently. "First of all, where were you last night when Stephanie died?"

Tania's eyes widened. "I was right here in the barracks. Stephanie sent me back here after I fell during maneuvers. My ankle really hurt, and I was so upset that I didn't want to see anybody. I didn't even go to the dance."

"Can you prove it?"

"Sure. We have to sign in and out at the lobby desk, and note the time as we come and go. You're welcome to check."

Tania got to her feet. "Why are you asking these questions, anyway? We all heard the detective say that Stephanie's death was an accident."

"I know. But I'm afraid I think she may have been killed, and I'm going to find out the facts." Even if the academy didn't exactly hire me to investigate, she added to herself.

"You don't think *I* wanted to kill her, do you?" Tania looked horrified. "I looked up to her, Nancy. I wanted to be just like her." The cadet's voice quivered. "I wanted to show Stephanie that I was Stafford material, that I could cut it." A tear rolled down Tania's cheek. "Now she's dead, and I'll never have that chance. I'll never get to prove myself to her."

Nancy laid a hand on the girl's arm. "I know how important she was to you," she said gently.

After a moment Tania stopped sobbing. "How can I help you?"

"Well, first you can tell me what you know about Stephanie's boyfriend. Do you know his name?"

Tania shook her head. "No, but I do know that Stephanie had been seeing someone for a couple of years. A civilian who goes to college part-time. He works in town."

"Did Stephanie ever talk about him?" Nancy asked. "Did she indicate trouble of any kind?"

"Not to me. But I saw her arguing with him a few times when he came to visit. They could get pretty ugly with each other," Tania said.

"Can you think of anyone who might know the name of Stephanie's boyfriend?"

"No," Tania said. "Stephanie didn't have a best friend. In fact, she didn't seem to have any friends at all. She was a real loner."

Nancy frowned. Finding out the boyfriend's name was going to be more difficult than she'd thought.

"What about other people who might have wanted to hurt Stephanie?"

"That's a tough one, Nancy. I think most cadets respected Stephanie, but a lot of them didn't like her much as a person. She pushed cadets to their limit, and sometimes she could be downright mean."

"Is there someone who stands out in your mind?" Nancy asked. "Think hard."

Tania was silent for a moment. "You know, there was someone: Joseph D'Angelo. He found out Stephanie had filed a report recommending his dismissal. He was furious. He came up to Stephanie when she was in the middle of a group of cadets and started screaming at her. I know he didn't mean it, but . . ."

Nancy prodded her. "But what?"

"He told Stephanie he'd kill her if it was the last thing he ever did."

Chapter

Seven

H E TOLD Stephanie that he'd *kill* her?" Nancy asked. "Are you sure those were his exact words?"

"I'm very sure." Tania laced her fingers together in her lap. "I'll never forget his expression when he said it." Tania looked at Nancy and lifted her chin. "Joseph was furious. He couldn't get Stephanie to back down, though. She didn't even flinch."

Nancy detected more than a trace of pride in Tania's voice.

"Does Joseph have a bad temper? Does he get into a lot of fights?"

"Well, he would fly off the handle pretty regularly—and he got in trouble for it a few times. But cadets keep arguments a secret. You can get lots of demerits for fighting."

Nancy's senses were on alert. "Do you have any idea where Joseph was last night? Was he at the dance?"

Tania shook her head. "No. He's not at the academy anymore."

"Why doesn't Joseph go to Stafford anymore?" Nancy asked, disappointed to lose a promising lead.

Tania bit her lip. "He left all of a sudden a few months ago. It was very hush-hush. Nothing official was ever said, but the rumor was that Stephanie caught him cheating on an exam and finally was able to get him thrown out."

Nancy raised her eyebrows. Joseph D'Angelo could be a promising lead after all. Perhaps the guy was mad enough to come back for revenge. It was certainly worth checking out.

"Do you know where I might find this guy?" Nancy asked.

"Sorry." Tania glanced at her watch. "Listen, I have someplace to go. Are you finished with me, Nancy?"

Nancy stood up. "I guess so. Thanks for your help, Tania," she said as the two girls left together.

In the elevator, Tania turned to Nancy. "If you have any more questions, or need help with anything, just ask."

"I may take you up on that, Tania," Nancy said. The two walked out into the brisk air. As they said their goodbyes, Nancy saw Trevor Austin leaning against a tree, watching them. When their eyes met, his lip curled into a contemptuous sneer. Nancy looked away and headed back to the hotel.

"Nancy, I don't even want to know how you got your hands on that sergeant's uniform," Nicholas said, leading Nancy up the walk toward Cardell Hall, where the records room was located.

Nancy glanced at him out of the corner of her eye and smiled. "You really don't."

Nicholas smiled back. "Well, I guess I do."

Nancy stood at attention. "It wasn't too hard, sir." She gave him a sharp salute. "The operation was completed by acquiring it from the laundry room, sir."

"You're too much." Nicholas shook his head.

As a cadet approached, Nicholas tapped Nancy once on the arm. It was a prearranged signal—one tap if the cadet was of higher rank and Nancy should salute first, two taps if the cadet was to salute her first.

Nancy raised her hand to her cap and held it there while the other cadet saluted and dropped his hand.

Nancy sighed with relief. If she messed up saluting other cadets, she was sure to be found out. And more important, Nicholas would be in deep trouble. The last thing she wanted was to jeopardize Nicholas's good reputation in any way. She was glad when they entered Cardell Hall and found the main corridor empty.

"We've got to be very careful," Nicholas whispered. "There might be someone in one of the offices."

Nancy was relieved they didn't run into anyone on their way to the records room. The building seemed deserted.

"I can't believe I'm doing this," Nicholas said as he fished a key from his pocket and unlocked the door. He looked into Nancy's eyes. "You must have me under some kind of spell."

"I must be under the same spell," Nancy murmured as she stepped inside.

The records room was small and musty. Row upon row of file cabinets covered the walls. Nicholas reached up and pulled a chain to turn on the single, unshaded lightbulb. Then he closed the door behind them.

"The files are separated into squads and arranged alphabetically," he said in a low voice. "Stephanie's squad is over here." Nancy felt the heat of his breath against her ear as he spoke.

He put his hand on Nancy's shoulder, and a flash of electricity shot through her. The next thing she knew, Nancy was in his arms looking up at his strong face as he gently brushed back her hair.

I must be crazy, Nancy thought. Then he softly pressed his mouth to hers, and Nancy closed her eyes and breathed deeply as she was swept into his kiss, her arms circling his neck.

Nicholas held her close and kissed her again, this kiss longer than the first. Nancy kissed him back for an instant, feeling wonderful and dizzy and breathless. Then a kaleidoscope of images broke the spell—Ned's face, Stephanie's cold lifeless body lying in the woods, Trevor's menacing sneer.

"Hey," Nicholas protested gently as she pulled away. "What's wrong?"

Nancy looked into his deep blue-gray eyes. She swallowed hard. "I think we forgot what we came here for." She tried to sound light, but she heard the tremor in her own voice. Most clearly, the image of Ned's face was etched firmly in her mind.

"Oh. Right." Nicholas released Nancy and stepped back. "Okay, let's start going through the files."

"Wait a minute." Nancy put her hand on his arm. "I think it might be better if I went through them alone. If we get caught in here together, you could be kicked out of the academy."

"I'm not leaving you here," Nicholas said emphatically.

"Nicholas, please." Nancy tapped her watch.

"There's no time to argue. I've done things like this before. I'm a detective, remember?"

Nicholas hesitated. "There probably won't be anyone around," he said after a moment. "All right, Nancy," he said as he reached for the doorknob. "But be careful."

Nancy watched as the door clicked shut. Then she grabbed the first file in Stephanie's squad and forced herself to focus on it.

The file belonged to a cadet named Steven Acheson. His grades were high. On his application he listed several awards from his former school as well as many extracurricular activities. The comments from his teachers, his coaches, and his advisor were very favorable.

Steven Acheson looks like a top-notch cadet so far, Nancy thought. Then she came to Stephanie Grindle's comments: "Steven needs to work on his attitude and take his training more seriously," she had written.

With such a glowing record, Stephanie's comments couldn't matter that much, Nancy thought. Her remarks were the only negative ones in the file, but they could easily hurt a less distinguished cadet.

The next folder belonged to Karen Adelman, whose record wasn't as brilliant as Steven's, but the remarks in her file were positive—except, it seemed, for Stephanie's. She blasted Karen for being sloppy and irresponsible and lacking team spirit.

By the time Nancy had read through a few more folders, her mind was reeling. Didn't anybody notice that Stephanie's was often the only negative report in a cadet's folder?

Nancy sighed. From the looks of things, it seemed just about anyone who knew Stephanie had a reason to be angry with her.

Then Nancy remembered Joseph D'Angelo, and she skipped ahead to his folder.

Joseph D'Angelo's photo showed a handsome face with dark hair, a strong jaw, and a smile that looked more like a smirk. Nancy thought she saw a mean look in his small, hard eyes.

His academic record was quite good, Nancy noticed. Did he earn those grades on his own, or did he get them by cheating? she wondered, flipping through the file to find a reference to the episode Tania had mentioned.

The more she read of the account of the incident, the less Nancy was convinced that anyone could be sure that he'd cheated. Stephanie had been proctoring the test in question. The charge of cheating had been brought on her word alone.

And the minutes from the Honor Board meeting showed that the decision to expel D'Angelo was the result of pressure from Stephanie.

Nancy found it disturbing that a cadet could be expelled with so little hard evidence. She found herself disliking Stephanie Grindle. The girl clearly liked to bully people, and her standards of fairness weren't very high.

Aside from the cheating incident, the only blots on Joseph D'Angelo's record were for fighting. He appeared to have an explosive temper. But did that mean he was capable of murder?

Nancy quickly scribbled Joseph D'Angelo's address. Since he lived in the next town, it would be easy for him to sneak back onto the campus. She made a mental note to pay Joseph a visit.

Just as Nancy replaced D'Angelo's file, she was startled by the sound of footsteps outside in the hallway. She heard voices, too, two men talking. The voices stopped just outside the door to the records room. Nancy could hear every word.

"I want this investigation wrapped up before the papers get hold of it," one voice was saying. "The last thing I need is a scandal at the school."

"Don't worry," the other voice, deep and gravelly, replied. "Everyone is convinced the whole thing was an accident, and my investigation will back that up. Soon we can release an official statement that there was no evidence of foul play and go about our business."

Nancy's heart beat faster. She recognized those voices. They belonged to Commander Royce and Detective Denman.

"I'm worried about that Nancy Drew. She's definitely the type to go sticking her nose into things," Commander Royce said.

"So get rid of her. Tell her she has to leave."

Commander Royce's voice sounded unsure. "Not yet. At this point she hasn't done anything. Telling her to leave would probably stir up trouble. She's the guest of our most distinguished cadet."

The detective laughed, a rough, rasping sound. "You really do worry too much, Martin. If you catch that girl snooping, *I'll* insist she leave the campus because she'll be interfering with a police investigation. Now, let's have a look at Stephanie Grindle's records."

Nancy could see the doorknob turning. She quickly scanned the room for a place to hide. She reached overhead and turned off the light. Standing in the middle of the records room, she held her breath and awaited her fate.

Chapter

Eight

THE DOOR to the records room clicked open, throwing a sliver of light along the floor. Nancy tiptoed behind a row of file cabinets and crouched down just as the door opened wide, bathing the room in light from the hallway.

Please don't come this way, Nancy begged silently. But the two men stood at the door talking. Nancy wondered if they were letting their eyes adjust to the dark inside the room. She knew it was only a matter of moments before they would turn on the overhead light and discover her.

"We have to make sure there's enough information about Stephanie Grindle in her file to make it look like there was nothing unusual about her going for a run by herself at night, even during a dance," Detective Denman said. "You know, notes from supervisors saying she's a loner, an overachiever, stuff like that."

"Well, there probably *is* that kind of information in her file," Commander Royce said. "She really did stick to herself."

Detective Denman laughed. "If it's not there, we'll put it there."

Nancy's eyes widened. Detective Denman was talking about manufacturing evidence—and Commander Royce was going along with him. She put her hand over her mouth as the light clicked on. She pressed herself against the file cabinet.

Then Nancy heard the sound of footsteps running in the hallway.

"Commander Royce!" Nancy heard the breathless voice of a female cadet. "There's a telephone call for you in your office. It's your wife. She told me to find you right away!"

"Right now?" The commander's voice was edged with annoyance.

"She said it was very important, sir," the cadet said.

"Oh, take the call," Detective Denman urged. "I'm hungry, anyway. We can do this later."

There was a moment of silence in the hall.

Nancy waited. Each second that dragged by seemed to be an hour.

Finally, the wedge of light became a sliver again. When Nancy heard the click of the door shutting, her knees went weak with relief. She listened to the sound of retreating footsteps.

"That was close," she whispered to herself.

When Nancy was sure the coast was clear, she slipped out of the records room and closed the door behind her. Then she hurried out of the building, head down, trying to look as inconspicuous as possible.

Why were they more interested in suppressing the investigation than getting to the truth? she wondered. Was it really just bad publicity the commander was worried about?

Nancy's first impulse was to go to the police and tell them everything, bring it all out into the open. But she didn't dare, because at this point it would be her word against that of Commander Royce and Detective Denman. It was better to keep everything to herself until she had some hard evidence.

"Hey, Nancy! Is that you? Wait up!" Nancy saw Bess and George hurrying toward her from across the lawn.

"Where did you disappear to, and why are you dressed like a cadet?" George demanded.

Nancy had forgotten she was wearing a

cadet's uniform. "Nicholas thought a disguise might help me do some investigating," she explained.

"Actually, it looks kind of cute on you, Nance," Bess said.

"Thanks." Nancy smiled and gave her friend a quick salute. "I was just looking at some cadet files in the records room."

"Why is it that we can't take Nancy anywhere without a case falling into her lap?" Bess asked.

George shook her head. "I've given up trying to figure that out," she said with a laugh. "Did you find anything, Nancy?"

Nancy was about to answer when an angry voice said, "What are you doing in that uniform, Nancy?"

Nancy whirled around and came face-to-face with Trevor Austin. "I just wanted see how I'd look as a cadet." She smiled as sweetly as she could.

"Oh, leave her alone, Trev. The lady makes a fine-looking cadet," said another boy who strode up beside Trevor.

Nancy's mouth dropped open. There was no mistaking the hard, dark eyes and the sneer lurking behind the smile. She recognized the boy from his picture. It was Joseph D'Angelo. And he was wearing a cadet's uniform!

"Anything wrong?" D'Angelo asked Nancy.

He smiled at her. It was the same twisted smirk she'd seen in the photo.

"You just remind me of someone, that's all," she managed to say.

"I hope it's someone you like," D'Angelo said in a honey-laced tone. He looked Nancy up and down. "I'd sure like to get to know *you* better."

"Come on, Joe, let's get out of here," Trevor snapped. "You don't want to bother with this one. She's trouble."

"Maybe I like trouble," Joseph said lazily. He shrugged and turned to follow Trevor. As he left, he looked at Nancy over his shoulder and mouthed the word "later."

"What a regular Romeo," Bess said.

"More like a regular sleazeball," George said.

"Well, to me he's a regular suspect," Nancy said. "Tania Allens told me he got into a fight with Stephanie and threatened to kill her. Whether or not he meant it or would do it is the question. But Tania also said he was thrown out for cheating."

"Well, it looks like he's back," Bess said.

Nancy nodded. "I've got to talk to Nicholas. Do you have any idea where he is?"

"Charlie said there was a rehearsal for the demonstration tomorrow," George said. "They're running through some drills on the playing field. Maybe he's there."

"I'd love to see the guys doing drills," Bess chimed in. "Let's go!"

"Not so fast," Nancy said. "I've got to get out of this uniform before anyone else recognizes me. I'll meet you there in a few minutes."

While Bess and George headed for the playing field, Nancy hurried back to the hotel, avoiding other cadets and trying to make herself as inconspicuous as possible.

In the hotel suite, Nancy looked in the mirror one more time before she took off the stiff, uncomfortable uniform. She couldn't imagine having to wear it every day. She put it in the back of the closet. Then she pulled on a thick sweater and jeans. In minutes she was on her way back to the playing field.

"That was quick!" George remarked as Nancy jogged up to them.

"I couldn't get out of that uniform fast enough," Nancy said breathlessly. She turned her attention to the cadets.

Nancy thought they looked impressive as they marched in formation. The most impressive of all was Nicholas, who marched at the head of the long lines of cadets, his head held high.

His voice shouted commands. "Right face! Company, halt!" Every cadet stood still.

"Dismissed!" The group disbanded in all directions. Nicholas headed straight for Nancy.

After a few minutes of small talk, George and Bess drifted away.

"I was worried about you," Nicholas said, taking both of Nancy's hands in his own. "If I didn't have to run the practice drill, I would have gone back to the records room. I could hardly keep my mind on what I was doing."

"You won't believe what happened—Commander Royce and Detective Denman almost caught me," Nancy said as they began walking around the playing field, "but the commander's wife called just before they came in the room."

"That was lucky," Nicholas said.

Nancy stopped walking and looked up at Nicholas. "I have to tell you something," she said. "Commander Royce isn't being honest about the investigation of Stephanie's death. I think he and Denman are plotting a cover-up. Royce said he was worried about bad publicity, but I'm not sure that's all there is to it."

"That's a pretty serious charge," Nick said.

"I overheard them talking about it, Nick. And you're right about Stephanie. Her reports seemed so negative and unfair that I'm sure she had a lot of enemies. And there's something else. Tania Allens told me Joseph D'Angelo was expelled for cheating—on Stephanie's recommendation. But I saw him in uniform today on campus."

Nicholas nodded. "I just found out that he's

been allowed to come back. He appealed his case directly to Commander Royce, and the commander overruled the decision of the Honor Board. It's very unusual."

Nancy's feet crunched against the cold ground as they began walking again. "Well, in this case, I think Commander Royce is right. From the information in D'Angelo's file, it looked as if Stephanie was out to get him."

Nicholas frowned. "I didn't think D'Angelo should have been expelled in the first place. There was nothing I could do about it, though. I had to go along with the decision of the Honor Board."

"Tania Allens also told me that D'Angelo had a fight with Stephanie and threatened to kill her."

Nicholas shook his head. "I can believe he said it. But I don't for a minute think he'd do it. Joe gets into fights, but he's no murderer. He just has a big mouth. He even threatened to kill me once!"

Nancy crossed her arms and looked at the ground. "I'm not ready to let go of Joseph D'Angelo as a suspect yet," she said. "But I need evidence." She thought for a moment. "Do you think you could help me get into Stephanie's room?"

Nicholas looked shocked. "Nancy! Haven't you done enough sneaking around already?

You've taken too many risks as it is. I don't think—"

Nancy interrupted. "Listen, I've just told you your commander is in on a cover-up." She put her hand on his arm. "I know you want to get to the bottom of this just as much as I do."

Nicholas was quiet.

"There might be something in Stephanie's room that will give us a lead," Nancy said quickly. "Please, Nick. We can't forget about the investigation now. We can solve this case— I just know it."

"Oh, all right." Nicholas's face opened into a wide grin. "I'm not sure you're a good influence on me. You've got me doing things I wouldn't have dreamed of before you arrived yesterday."

Nancy smiled. "Thanks, Nick." She was touched that Nicholas was so willing to go out on a limb for her.

"Let's think for a minute," Nicholas said.

Nancy's heart fluttered as she watched him. The long weekend was flying by. She only had two more days to solve the case—and two more days to get to know Nicholas. She didn't want to think about what would happen when she had to go back home.

"I know this much," Nicholas said. "I'm not going to let you go into Stephanie's room by yourself. This time, I'm going with you."

"That's fine with me," Nancy said.

Usually, she liked to work alone, but for Nicholas she was willing to make an exception.

"They're having the jeans party tonight," Nicholas said, thinking out loud as he paced back and forth.

Nancy nodded. She remembered George telling her about the casual party the day after the formal, when even the cadets wore jeans.

"Everyone will be having a good time," Nicholas said, "and you and I can probably slip out without being noticed. That's got to be your best chance to search Stephanie's room."

"Great!" Nancy had a hunch that when she searched Stephanie's room, she'd find the clue she'd been looking for.

"I'm not quite as enthusiastic as you are," Nicholas said. "I was looking forward to spending time with you at the party."

"I was looking forward to spending time with you, too," Nancy said. "Our search won't take long. We'll have plenty of time at the party. Anyway, the sooner I solve this case, the better. Then we can spend much more time together."

"Now, that's something I can get enthusiastic about," Nicholas said. He glanced at his watch. "I've got to help the decorating committee get ready for the party. I'll see you later, okay?" He put his hands on Nancy's shoulders and leaned toward her with a quick kiss.

"See you later," Nancy said. She watched

Nicholas walk away. This weekend isn't very long, she told herself, and I'm going to have fun. I'll sort out my feelings later.

After Nicholas left, Nancy headed for the hotel. A cadet fell into step beside her. Nancy was startled to see it was Joseph D' Angelo. He studied her face with undisguised hostility.

"So you're Nancy Drew, the detective."

Nancy nodded. "What's the matter? Don't you like me now that you know my name, Cadet D'Angelo?" She gave him a sly smile. "How's your reinstatement going?"

Joseph's lip curled. "I'm not surprised that you know who I am. Trevor told me all about you, how you're sticking your nose in and asking questions about Stephanie's death. The police already said it looked like an accident. And I'd really like to know what makes *you* think *I* killed Stephanie."

Nancy stopped walking and faced Joseph. "I just want to find out what really happened."

D'Angelo looked as if he was about to lose his temper. "Just mind your own business," he hissed before walking away.

Nancy watched him go. He's slimy, she thought as she rubbed the back of her neck. Every muscle in her body was tight with tension, and she couldn't wait to get into a hot bath. She broke into a jog and kept running until she got to the hotel.

As she stepped off the elevator on her floor, she saw Tania Allens standing by her door, looking as if she was about to faint. Her hand was covered with blood.

Chapter

Nine

TAKE IT EASY, Tania. The cut may not be so bad," Nancy said as she led a frightened Tania into her room. Once she had washed the blood away, all that was left on Tania's hand was a small wound.

"It was the way I got cut that scared me," Tania said. Color began returning to her pale face. She held out a bloodstained note for Nancy to read.

The paper was covered with letters cut from newspapers and magazines assembled to form a single threatening sentence: "YOU'D BETTER STOP HELPING 'DETECTIVE' DREW!"

"I found the note in an envelope under my door," Tania said. "I guess there was a razor blade inside the envelope, too, and I cut myself when I reached in and pulled out the note."

Nancy's eyes narrowed. Trevor Austin knew I wanted to question Tania, and he saw us together when we left her dorm, she thought. Did he put the note under Tania's door to frighten her away from cooperating further?

"Did you see anyone hanging around when you went into the room and found the note?" Nancy asked.

Tania shook her head, then she lifted her chin. "I'm not going to let this scare me," she said. "I still want to help you, Nancy."

"Thanks, Tania," Nancy said. "But I think we should be careful about being seen together. I wouldn't want anything to happen to you."

"Don't worry, Nancy. I'll be careful," Tania said as she walked to the door. Nancy was impressed by her calm resolve. Perhaps Tania wasn't so fragile after all.

After Tania left, Nancy folded the threatening message and tucked it inside her notebook. She began mentally to check off her suspects once again. Which one of them could have done this?

Nancy's thoughts were interrupted when Bess and George came into the room. "Something has happened. I can tell by the look on your face," George said as she and Bess settled into chairs.

"You're right," Nancy said. "Tania Allens just got a threatening note telling her not to help me. There was a razor blade inside the envelope, and she cut herself on it."

Bess gasped. "Is she badly hurt?"

Nancy shook her head. "It was just a scratch, but she was pretty shaken up over it." Nancy sat down on her bed.

"Any idea who did it?" George asked.

"I'm not sure, but Trevor is a distinct possibility," Nancy said. "For some reason he doesn't want me asking questions about Stephanie's death. He's been very clear about that."

Bess groaned. "Trevor keeps showing up like a bad penny wherever I go, wanting to talk to me. I wish he'd leave me alone," she said wearily.

"I hate to spoil your fun, Bess, but it would help a lot if you would see what Trevor has to say," Nancy said.

"Right," George agreed. "If you talk to him, you might find out something useful."

Bess let out a long sigh. "I suppose you're right. I can talk to him tonight at the party."

Several hours later the girls stood at the entrance to the main dining room in Rosamond Hall, where the party was being held. All three were wearing jeans and sweaters.

Nancy surveyed the room. The ceiling had been draped with a parachute, which made it look as if it were covered with billowy clouds.

Several small, round tables and chairs stood in one corner near the refreshment stand. Each table held a candle in the center. Chairs were placed against the walls all around the room, leaving space for a huge dance area in the center.

"I can't wait to dance," Bess said. The band was playing a loud rock tune.

Nancy felt a tap on her shoulder. She turned and looked into Nicholas's deep blue-gray eyes. "You look great," he said.

"You, too," Nancy whispered.

Nicholas quickly took Nancy's hand. "Come on, let's dance," he said to her. "The party is just starting." Then he leaned closer and whispered in her ear: "It would look suspicious if we left right away."

"I absolutely agree," Nancy said.

"Are you still interested in me now that I'm wearing jeans, or was it just the uniform that turned your head?" Nicholas joked as he led Nancy to the dance floor.

"I don't know," Nancy joked back. "Let's see if you dance as well in jeans as you do in uniform."

Nancy watched Nicholas move to the beat of the music. She had to admit, she liked the way he looked in his uniform. But he looked even better in casual clothes.

Nicholas danced closer to Nancy. He reached

out and swept her hair away from her ear. "So, do I pass inspection, ma'am?" he said loud enough for only her to hear.

Before Nancy had a chance to answer him, the band began a sweet slow song, and Nicholas pulled Nancy into his arms and held her close.

"I wish this weekend would never end," Nicholas said, leaning down to kiss her gently on her lips.

As Nancy felt his lips brush hers, she wondered how she could have fallen for him so quickly. Thoughts of Ned began tying her stomach in knots.

"What's wrong?" Nicholas looked confused as he sensed the shift in Nancy's feelings.

Nancy looked away. "I think this might be a good time for us to slip out of the party and over to Stephanie's room," she said. "I have to keep reminding myself to concentrate on the investigation."

"I don't think it's a good idea right now," Nicholas said. He leaned down and whispered in her ear. "Trevor Austin is watching our every move."

Nancy looked up after a moment and casually scanned the room. Trevor was standing in a corner by himself, staring at her and Nicholas. "He seems to know we've got something planned," she said. "But I think I know how to distract him. Wait for me by the refreshment stand."

As Nancy broke away from Nicholas, Trevor followed her with his eyes. She headed straight for the ladies' room, the one place she knew he couldn't follow.

In the ladies' room, Nancy ran into George. "You and Nicholas seem to be enjoying yourselves," George said with a grin.

"Yes," Nancy said in a hushed voice, "but the plan was for the two of us to slip out of the party and then to search Stephanie's room for clues. We can't, though, because Trevor is watching us like a hawk."

"Trevor Austin is looking more and more suspicious himself," George said as she pulled a small brush from her purse.

Nancy nodded her agreement. "Now's the time for Bess to distract him. Can you find her and explain the situation?"

"Sure," George said. She quickly smoothed the brush through her hair and put it away. "I'll track Bess down right now."

Moments later, Nancy passed Trevor as she left the ladies' room. He followed her back to the refreshment table where Nicholas was waiting, then stood several feet away, doing nothing to disguise the fact that he was watching them.

Nancy helped herself to a cold bottle of

spring water. "Plan A to distract Trevor is now in action," she whispered to Nicholas. "We just have to be patient."

As it happened, they didn't have to wait long. Soon Nancy saw George talking to Bess. After a few minutes, Bess walked over to Trevor. He looked clearly surprised to see her approach.

Nancy watched as Bess inconspicuously positioned her body so that Trevor had to turn his back to Nancy and Nicholas. Soon Bess and the cadet were deep in conversation.

"Come on, let's make our move," Nancy whispered.

Nicholas nodded silently. He took Nancy's hand and led her across the crowded dance floor to the back entrance of Rosamond Hall.

Soon they were heading across the dark campus in the direction of the barracks. As they walked, Nancy kept glancing over her shoulder. She wasn't sure how long Bess could keep Trevor occupied. She half expected to see him rushing after them at any moment.

"Stephanie's room was on the first floor in Barracks B," Nicholas told Nancy as they hurried along. "At this time of night, there are no cadets on duty, but we'll still have to slip by the regular guard at the desk. If we're lucky, though, and the window is unlocked, we might be able to slip in."

Nancy knew it was likely that Stephanie's

room had been sealed off after she died. Still, they *could* hope for a miracle, she thought.

The walkway leading to the dorm was brightly lit. Fortunately, Stephanie's room faced the back. Nicholas and Nancy were careful to make as little noise as possible as they crept to the rear of the building.

"Stephanie was in room seventeen," Nicholas whispered. "Over here."

He stopped at a window and reached up to open it.

It didn't budge.

Nicholas tried again. The window frame moved a fraction of an inch with a squeak that made them both jump.

"Is it locked?" Nancy asked.

Nicholas shook his head. "I think it's just stuck. But it's not moving. And if we make any more noise, someone is bound to hear us."

"Let me try," Nancy whispered. Back home, she was known to have just the right touch with hard-to-open jars and doors. Better hope I've got the magic touch right now, she thought.

Nancy placed both hands under the top edge of the window and pushed up gently. Then she jiggled the window frame a little and pushed again. Then she jiggled and pushed once more. In this way, she was able to open the window a tiny bit at a time. Getting the window open wide enough to fit a body through took several minutes, but to Nancy and Nicholas it seemed like hours.

"I did it," Nancy said finally. "I think we can make it." She threw her leg over the windowsill and bent over double to squeeze through the opening. It was an even tighter fit for Nicholas, but in a moment the two of them were standing inside Stephanie's room.

"We should have brought flashlights," Nicholas said.

Nancy nearly let out a giggle. "Don't you think we would have looked awfully suspicious leaving the dance with flashlights?" she asked. "I don't think even Bess could have distracted Trevor from *that* sight."

"I guess you're right." Nicholas laughed softly. "Stand here while I turn on the light."

Nancy waited, her heart hammering. When the room was bathed in light, she gasped. Someone had already searched Stephanie's room. Searched it so thoroughly, in fact, that it was completely trashed!

Chapter

Ten

NANCY AND NICHOLAS gazed in amazement at the disaster that was Stephanie's room. Neither of them could speak.

Every dresser drawer had been emptied of its contents. Books had been thrown out of the bookcase, and the desk was on its side with papers strewn everywhere.

The closet doors stood open. Clothes and shoes lay scattered on the floor, and the sheets had been torn from the bed.

"If there was anything here to find, it's probably long gone by now," Nicholas said, looking around at the mess.

"Let's give it a try," Nancy said as she knelt to look under the bed.

"I'm game," Nicholas said. "But what exactly are we looking for?"

Nancy smiled. "I'll know when I find it."

"Give me a hint, then," Nicholas said, playfully punching Nancy's arm.

"Something like a letter or a diary, or maybe notes she made to herself about one of the cadets," Nancy said. "I'm looking for something that will give me a clue about who might have hated Stephanie enough to kill her."

Nicholas nodded. Before he started to look, he paused for a moment and turned to Nancy. "You don't think the police made this mess, do you?" he asked.

"I can't say for sure," Nancy said. "Denman wasn't interested in searching for evidence at the crime scene. I doubt he'd make the effort to take apart a room. I think it's more likely that the killer did this."

The two split up the search; Nicholas rifled through notebooks while Nancy searched through the clothing and more personal items. Nicholas turned the desk upright and checked the backs of the drawers while Nancy searched the bureau.

An hour later neither one of them had come up with anything.

"It's kind of scary that Stephanie didn't seem to keep anything personal around. There aren't any letters or pictures at all," Nicholas said.

"Unless someone took them already," Nancy

said. Then something caught her eye. It was a piece of paper caught between the bed frame and the box spring. She picked it up. It was an envelope with a letter inside.

Nancy unfolded the letter and quickly scanned the pages. It was immediately clear to her that the letter was from Stephanie's boyfriend and that he wasn't happy with her. Over and over, he mentioned her selfishness and her driving ambition. " 'I'll get back at you one day for what you've done to me,' " Nancy read aloud. The tone was so threatening that a shiver ran up Nancy's back.

On the last page, Nancy saw that the letter was signed "John."

Was Stephanie involved in an abusive relationship? Nancy wondered. From the looks of things, the writer was definitely disturbed— and possibly angry enough to do something rash.

Nancy peered inside the envelope again and found some torn scraps of paper. She took them out and cleared a space on the bed. She carefully fit the scraps together like pieces of a jigsaw puzzle. When she was done, she stared into a photograph of Stephanie and a tall guy with dark hair and piercing blue eyes. They appeared to be a happy couple, dressed up and smiling for the camera.

"Look at this," Nancy said. "This has got to be John with her. Now, if only there were a return address on the envelope . . ."

"We should get going, Nancy," Nicholas said. "It's getting late, and we've been gone from the party for more than an hour."

Nancy nodded. She slipped the letter and the pieces of the photograph into her pocket, and the two of them slipped out the window.

Nancy and Nicholas walked slowly back to the party in the moonlight. They had to get back to the party, but Nancy didn't want to rush. She looked up at Nicholas's strong profile and thought of the small adventure they'd just had together. She had liked searching Stephanie's room with him. It was exciting, and so was he, she decided with mixed emotions. She didn't quite know how he was going to fit into her life.

Nancy looked up at the stars. The only thing she *did* know was that she didn't want to leave Nicholas, not yet.

When they got back to the party, Bess and Trevor were dancing. Bess caught Nancy's eye and gave her a look that said, "You owe me big time."

Nancy waved and smiled at Bess as if she'd only been gone for a minute. Then she and

Nicholas joined the others on the dance floor and danced until the party was over.

On Sunday morning Nancy was up early. She took the pieces of the photograph of Stephanie and John that she had found in Stephanie's room and taped them together, then headed over to see Tania. She found Tania in her room putting on her jacket.

"Morning, Nancy," Tania said with a smile. "I was just about to go get breakfast. Want to join me?"

Nancy shook her head. "We aren't going to be seen together if we can help it, remember, Tania? I mean, after you got that note about staying away from me."

"Oh, right," Tania said with an embarrassed laugh.

Nancy thought it was strange that Tania seemed suddenly so unconcerned. She had been so terrified the day before.

"Have you had any more threats?" Nancy asked.

Tania hesitated. "Well, not in writing. But I think someone has been following me."

"Who?" Nancy asked.

Tania reddened. "Well, I haven't actually gotten a look at anyone. It's just an uneasy feeling I have."

Nancy wondered if Tania was really being followed or if she was a very good actress.

She showed Tania the taped-together photograph. "Have you ever seen Stephanie with this guy?"

Tania looked at the picture, and her face registered shock. "Where did you get this?"

"You'd be surprised how things turn up in an investigation," Nancy said. She wasn't about to tell Tania about sneaking into Stephanie's room.

"Well, it's Stephanie's boyfriend, all right," Tania said.

"And you're sure you don't remember his name?" Nancy asked.

Tania shook her head. "Like I said, all I know is that he and Stephanie fought a lot." Tania tilted her head to one side. "Does that help?"

Not much, Nancy thought. Aloud she said, "Everything helps, Tania. Thanks."

"I've reached another dead end," Nancy told Bess and George in the main dining room over breakfast. "I haven't the faintest idea of how to locate this boyfriend. His name is John, but John who?"

Bess and George couldn't help Nancy with that. But Bess had some interesting things to say about her talk with Trevor at the party the night before.

"Trevor was very apologetic," Bess said. "He actually sounded really sorry about the way he'd acted and for the things he'd said about women. Then we danced. He *is* a great dancer, although I don't agree with Charlie that he's the best dancer at Stafford Academy."

Bess helped herself to a cinnamon danish. "I was just about ready to forgive Trevor," she went on. "Then he started asking questions."

Nancy raised her eyebrows. "About what?"

"You, mostly. He wanted to know if you were still 'poking around,' as he said, trying to find out about Stephanie's death, and whether you'd found anything. I didn't tell him a thing, Nan. I said you were too caught up with Nicholas, and you were leaving the investigation to the police."

"Thanks, Bess." Nancy buttered a piece of toast.

"No problem," Bess said. "The only thing is, I'm not sure he believed me."

"Why not?" Nancy asked.

Bess frowned. "I can't say exactly. He just didn't look completely convinced. Maybe I went overboard in describing just how head over heels in love with Nicholas you are," she added playfully.

"I hate to interrupt," George said before Nancy could answer, "but the cadets are performing their demonstration on the parade grounds in ten minutes." She looked at Nancy.

"And a certain dashing young battalion commander—or shall I say knight in shining armor—will be leading them."

"I can't wait to see the mounted troops perform afterward," Bess said.

"Enough, you two." Nancy stood up to return her tray. "Come on!"

The sun was bright, and the air was crisp on the parade grounds. The crowd was just beginning to assemble when Nancy, Bess, and George arrived.

Nancy was surprised when a cadet stepped up and asked her if she was Nancy Drew.

"Yes," Nancy answered. "Why?"

The cadet snapped out a salute. "Battalion Commander Dufont has instructed me to escort you and your friends to the elite viewing area."

"Thank you." Nancy couldn't help smiling as the three of them followed the cadet to an area just above the far end of the grounds. A crowd of about a hundred people stood there under a canopy at the edge of the field.

"The parade passes here first," the cadet told them. "You'll be right up front."

"What happens now, I wonder?" Nancy asked as the cadet led them to the front of the crowd.

"Charlie told me that first the different companies perform their drills," George answered.

"Then the mounted troops ride a loop around the grounds, and they do some drills of their own on horseback."

"I can't wait," Nancy said, wondering where Nicholas was.

She felt someone bump her heel. "Sorry," said the man behind her. "It's so crowded."

"That's okay," Nancy replied, and took a step forward to give herself more room—and a better view of Nicholas, she thought.

Then the parade started. First came the band, playing a rousing march. When the marching stopped, an announcement was heard over the loudspeaker. "Presenting Battalion Commander Captain Nicholas Dufont!"

Nicholas rode out, sitting straight and tall on a magnificent bay horse. He was wearing his full-dress uniform and an extremely tall hat with a single burgundy feather.

Nicholas saluted the crowd. Then the announcer's voice said, "And now the battalion."

A cheer rose from the crowd. Line after line of marching cadets passed by. Nancy couldn't believe how regal Nicholas looked commanding the troops. He led company after company in drills, marching in formation. When Nicholas and the troops left the field, a line of high-stepping horses trotted out, their necks arched proudly and their coats gleaming in the sun.

Most of the horses behaved beautifully, following the silent commands of their riders. Yet a bay stallion in the middle of the line was acting a little skittish. It kept sidestepping and throwing its head up in the air.

As the line of horses paraded past the spectators, the bay continued to act up. It kicked its back legs out and nearly hit the horse behind it.

"If that rider can't control his horse, he ought to take it out of the line," George said disapprovingly.

No sooner were the words out of her mouth than the horse neighed and reared up on its back legs. A cry of alarm surged through the crowd. The noise seemed to excite the horse even more. It reared again and shook its head. As soon as its front hooves came down on the dirt, it took off at a gallop. The rider pulled back hard on the reins, but the stallion had taken the bit and was racing out of control.

Charging toward the edge of the field where the crowd stood under the canopy, horse and rider seemed to be heading straight for Nancy. As the horse approached, she could see that its rider was none other than Joseph D'Angelo. In a moment she would be trampled under its hooves.

Chapter

Eleven

Nancy tried to twist out of the horse's path, but the crowd was too tightly packed behind her. The horse seemed to gain speed, D'Angelo leaning far forward like a jockey.

As the horse came closer and closer, Nancy could see the wild look in its eyes. It was impossible to avoid it, and Nancy did something that made the crowd gasp. She moved forward, *into* the horse's path. She waved her arms in wide arcs in front of her and shouted, "Back! Back!"

The bay stopped short, reared on its hind legs, and neighed loudly. Its hooves thumped down on the ground inches from Nancy's feet. She could see the sweat foaming white along its neck and feel its hot breath on her face. The horse reared again. Once more the hooves narrowly missed her face.

Cadets came running from all directions. Charlie and Nicholas were the first to reach the horse. They each grabbed a side of the bridle and hung on as the horse pulled them several yards. Other cadets moved in to calm the crowd.

It took some time, but the horse finally stopped its frantic movements. To a casual observer, Joseph D'Angelo appeared to have lost control of the horse, but Nancy knew otherwise. She had been around horses enough to know Joseph knew just what he was doing.

Charlie walked the horse from the parade grounds with the help of two mounted cadets. Bess and George rushed up to Nancy and threw their arms around her.

"Thank goodness you're all right," Bess said in a choked voice.

George's face was pale. "That could have been a horrible scene."

Nancy took several deep breaths before she spoke. "I'm not sure that was an accident. I recognized the rider. It was Joseph D'Angelo."

Nicholas ran over and put his hands on Nancy's shoulders. "That was a close call," he said gravely.

Nancy could see how upset he was. "I'm all

right, Nicholas," she said reassuringly. "It was scary, but I'm not hurt."

"Isn't that horse too high-strung to be performing in front of a crowd?" George demanded.

Nicholas nodded. "Well, now we know it is. I'll have to look into its training. It clearly wasn't ready to face such a big crowd."

He gazed at Nancy tenderly. "I should have told some cadets to stand near you in case anything happened," he said.

Nancy shook her head. "It's not your fault. Who could have known this would happen?"

The conversation was interrupted by a voice over the loudspeakers, announcing a short intermission.

"I think I've had enough excitement for today," Bess said. "How about you, George?"

"I'm going to head over to the stable and see what's going on," George replied. "Want to come, Nancy?"

Nancy nodded. "Absolutely. Let's get going."

Nicholas put a restraining hand on Nancy's arm. "Hey, Nancy, that doesn't sound like a good idea."

"Why not?" she asked.

"Well, for one thing, you were nearly trampled by a horse just now. You should probably get some rest."

Nancy frowned. "I don't need any rest. I'm fine, really." She began walking toward the stables. "Come on, George," she said.

Nicholas stepped in front of her. "Nancy, I really don't think you should go."

Nancy felt a tide of irritation welling up inside her. "Please, Nicholas," she said tightly. She wasn't sure if he was being caring or controlling, but she was too weary to think about it.

"Maybe he's right, Nancy," George said. "I can find out what caused the horse to get spooked. I've been to the stables already, so I know my way around."

Nancy hesitated. She *was* feeling a little unsteady, and her head had begun to ache with tension. "All right, George. You go to the stables. Keep your eyes and ears open, and tell me everything you find out."

"You know I will," George said as she turned to walk away.

"I'll come to the stables after I've taken Nancy back to her room," Nicholas called after her. He put his arm around Nancy and steered her toward the hotel.

"If I find out that Joseph D'Angelo let that horse go out of control, he'll wish he never came back to Stafford," Nicholas said, his voice trembling with anger. "The Honor Board won't have anything to do with what happens to him, either."

The remark took Nancy by surprise. So he shared her conviction that what had happened was no accident.

"Nicholas, the last time we talked about Joseph D'Angelo, you thought he was the kind of guy who flew off the handle sometimes but mostly just made empty threats. What's made you change your mind?"

Nicholas looked uncomfortable. "I didn't like the way that horse charged right at you. Joseph D'Angelo is an accomplished rider. Even with a skittish horse, he should have been able to keep it from galloping into the crowd."

"I agree with you. I saw the determined look in his eye. But let's not jump to conclusions," Nancy said. "I'd like to question him about what happened and about Stephanie, but I don't think he'll talk to me. He seems to think I'm trying to frame him. Any ideas?"

Nicholas nodded his head rapidly. "Yes, I've got a *really* good idea. Stop this investigation before you get yourself killed."

Nancy heard the tension in his voice. He was afraid for her. "I understand how you feel, Nicholas, but I can't stop. I'll be careful, I promise."

When Nicholas dropped Nancy off at the

hotel, he kissed her gently. "I'll be back later," he said. "Try to rest."

In the hotel room, Nancy savored the memory of his kiss as she drifted into a fitful sleep. She tossed and turned for just about an hour, before she was awakened by voices. Bess and George had returned and were talking softly.

"Speak up, you two. I can't hear you when you whisper like that," Nancy said as she sat up in bed. "Did you find out anything at the stable, George?"

George plopped down into a chair and stretched her long legs out in front of her. "When I got there, Charlie said he'd already checked everything out. The saddle and bridle hadn't been tampered with, and the horse seemed perfectly healthy. He said they were going to have a veterinarian examine the horse, but as far as Charlie was concerned, there was no foul play. The horse is just high-strung."

"High-strung is one thing, homicidal is another," Bess muttered.

"I'll say," George said. "Listen to what I heard from the assistant riding master. Joseph D'Angelo was told specifically *not* to take that horse out. It was a direct order from the riding master. He wanted that horse so badly, though, he sneaked it out when the riding master was at the parade. Then he lied to the assistant, saying that the riding master had changed his mind."

Bess sat down beside Nancy. "I went with George, and I heard the whole thing." She sighed. "I feel sorry for the assistant. He's in trouble now, too, and it really wasn't his fault. He was beside himself over what happened."

George crossed her arms over her chest. "Well, they were both really sorry when Nicholas showed up and found out what happened. Charlie told me it was the closest he's ever seen Nicholas come to losing his temper."

"You know, I guess it could just be Joseph D'Angelo's stupid attempt to show off," Nancy said.

George shook her head. "I don't think so. I talked to a couple of cadets who think that he should have been able to control that horse."

"That's what Nicholas thought," Nancy mused. "And that's what I thought."

The phone rang, and George got up to answer it. "It's Charlie," she mouthed silently. Bess and Nancy waited while George listened, nodding her head every so often.

"Wait until you hear this," she said, and sat down on Nancy's bed. "Charlie said he caught D'Angelo trying to empty the horse's water trough. He'd been told not to touch it until after the veterinarian tested it for drugs. Joseph told Charlie to mind his own business, but Charlie had a chance to smell the water. He thought it smelled weird, so he put just a drop on his tongue. He said it was bitter. Something definitely had been added to it."

"It sounds like we're onto something," Nancy said. "I hate to just sit around waiting for the test results, though. I wonder what my next move should be."

"Forget about the case for a moment, Nancy," George said. "What about your next move with Nicholas? I could see how upset he was today. I think he's really in love with you."

"I agree with George," Bess said. "You can practically feel it in the air when you two are together."

"I wish I knew what to do." Nancy sighed. "I'm still in love with Ned, but when I'm around Nicholas, well, something just *happens*. I don't want to be attracted to any other guy, but I can't help it. Nick is so—"

The phone rang again.

"I wonder who that could be," Bess said with a sly smile.

George laughed. "It's Ned, calling to check up on you."

"Very funny," Nancy said as she reached for the phone. "He doesn't have the number. But maybe I should call him. It might help sort out my feelings."

"Hello?" she said into the receiver.

There was no answer.

Someone's playing games, Nancy thought. "Hello?" she said once more before deciding to hang up.

Then a muffled voice at the other end spoke with great urgency. "Nancy Drew, you're in danger."

Chapter

Twelve

"WHO IS THIS?" Nancy demanded sharply. She signaled to Bess and George, and they sat on either side, leaning close to listen in.

"I'm sorry," the caller said. "I didn't mean to scare you. My name is John Greenman."

He paused. "I was Stephanie Grindle's boyfriend, and I've been trying to track you down. I think you're in danger."

Nancy wondered if this was a stroke of luck or a setup. "I'm glad you called, John," she said slowly, exchanging puzzled looks with Bess and George. "I wanted to talk to you, too. Can we meet?"

"Yes," John said. "Tonight, if possible, at eight o'clock. I don't want to come to the campus; I'll explain why later. Do you know the bus stop on Lundsford Road?"

Nancy remembered seeing a bus shelter as they'd driven into the academy. "Yes, I know it."

"Okay, I'll park my car—it's a dark blue sedan—at the bus stop. I'll blink the lights when I see you."

"Fine," Nancy said. "I'll be wearing—"

"Never mind," the voice interrupted. "I know who you are."

"It's too risky, Nan," Bess said when Nancy hung up. "Don't go."

"I know it's dangerous," Nancy said. "But it's our only real lead, and I have to follow it." Nancy looked at her two worried friends. "Besides," she added, "I think John Greenman is smart enough to know he'd be pointing a finger at himself if he tried anything."

Nancy paced the room for a minute, thinking of questions she was going to ask Greenman. Then she turned to her friends.

"Listen, you guys," she said. "Don't say anything about this to Nicholas. I'm going to have a hard enough time keeping him from—"

Nancy was interrupted by a knock at the door. When she opened it, Nicholas was standing on the other side.

"Hi, Nicholas. Come in." Nancy could tell that he was angry.

Nicholas glanced at Bess and George, then looked at Nancy. He tapped the door with his index finger. "These doors aren't very thick, I'm afraid. I was standing right outside just now. What is it that you want to keep from me?"

"I'm going to arrive late at the dance tonight," Nancy said. "I have to meet someone first."

"Nancy, you can't act this way. I need to know who you're meeting," Nicholas demanded.

"I can't tell you yet," she said to him. "I just want to concentrate on solving this case."

"Don't do it, whatever it is," Nicholas said. "I don't want anything to happen to you. I'm worried, Nan. Especially after what happened today."

Nancy shook her head. "I know I can solve this case," she said. "I can't just stop investigating at the slightest hint of danger."

Bess and George silently excused themselves and stepped outside the room.

"I forbid you to have any more involvement with this murder investigation," Nicholas said, standing squarely in front of her.

Nancy's eyes flashed defiantly. "You can't *forbid* me to do anything. I'm not one of the cadets under your command."

Nicholas looked at her with sad eyes. Without another word, he started for the door.

Nancy watched him in silence as feelings

welled inside her. Letting him go wrenched her heart, but her head told her she had to. Though his protectiveness was flattering, she had begun to feel confined by it.

Just as Nicholas was about to step out the door, he turned around. Nancy's breath caught in her throat. From the look in his eyes, she thought for a moment he was going to come back, take her in his arms, and kiss her.

Then Nicholas whirled back around and was gone. As the door closed behind him, Nancy breathed a sigh of regret mixed with relief.

After a moment, Bess and George returned. "Is everything all right, Nan?" George asked softly.

Nancy took a deep breath. "Not exactly, George, but I'm not going to think about it right now. I have a case to solve."

At 7:50 that evening, Nancy walked purposefully across the campus. She pulled the collar of her jacket tightly around her neck. A wind had blown up and was rustling the branches of the trees. Nancy walked nearly a mile down the access road that led to the main entrance to the academy.

As she passed the gates, the sight of the guardhouse brought her up short. It was empty. Nancy had taken it for granted that the guardhouse was staffed at all times.

She walked past the gates and turned in the direction of the bus shelter. I didn't realize it would be so deserted this early in the evening, she thought as she looked at the lonely stretch of road. The bus shelter was farther from the gates than she had remembered.

Standing there alone, she looked back at the academy. For an instant a rush of fear rose inside her. With the safety of Stafford in the distance, she wasn't as confident as she had been earlier. Maybe I shouldn't be doing this, she thought.

Up ahead she saw a car beam flash through the darkness once and then again. Nancy took a deep breath. "You've come this far, Drew," she whispered, "you can't stop now." She moved toward the lights.

The car door on the driver's side opened, and a man got out and walked toward her.

Nancy continued forward. "John?" she asked. Then, as she got closer, her heart began to pound. The person she saw was middle-aged, short, and powerfully built, not lean and lanky like the young man in the photograph.

Sensing danger, Nancy backed away, then turned and ran toward the safety of the academy.

Behind her she heard a voice call out, "Nancy, wait!" Then two sets of footsteps came running toward her.

"Wait!" the voice called again. "We're not here to hurt you." Nancy slowed down. She recognized that voice.

"I'm John Greenman. This man is my boss."

That's the voice I heard on the telephone, Nancy realized. She stopped and turned around. Standing before her was the young man from the picture.

"Why didn't you come alone?" Nancy asked. "You scared the daylights out of me."

"I made him bring me," the older man said. "I'm Mike Ramsey, from the *Union Dispatch News.*"

Nancy recognized the name instantly. Mike Ramsey was a famous journalist, known for sniffing out newsworthy stories in unlikely places.

"Why are you here, Mr. Ramsey?"

John Greenman spoke up. "Let's just go have a cup of coffee somewhere, and I'll explain."

"All right," Nancy agreed. She got in the car, no longer frightened. This better be good, she thought angrily. A reporter is the last thing I need right now.

"I'm on the staff of the *Union Dispatch News* as a journalism intern," John explained once they were seated at a diner in town. "Mike is my supervisor. When I got suspicious about Stephanie's death, I told him about it." He paused to take a sip of coffee.

"Stephanie was supposed to meet me the day after we had a big fight in the parking lot. But she never showed up. I called her several times and kept getting her answering machine. When she didn't return my calls, I contacted the academy administration."

"What did they say?" Nancy asked.

"They told me about the accident," John said. "I didn't believe it, though. Stephanie was a fantastic runner. She had run that course a million times. She wouldn't have slipped on gravel or wet leaves or anything—even at night. I'm sure of it. I think she was killed. That's what you think, too, isn't it?"

Nancy was surprised at the sudden question. "Well, I suppose I'm not ready to believe that it was an accident just yet. Do you know why anyone would want to kill Stephanie?"

John Greenman surprised her by slamming his fist on the table and saying, "Yes! I think Stephanie was killed because she knew too much."

Nancy's eyes narrowed. "Knew too much about what?"

John's voice was cold. "I'm not sure, but I have a few ideas. I got them when I saw Joseph D'Angelo on campus the other day."

"What do you know about Joseph D'Angelo?" Nancy asked.

"Only that Stephanie thought he was involved in something funny going on at the academy. She had caught him cheating, but there was more to it than that."

John leaned across the table toward Nancy. "I think that he killed Stephanie because she found something out. And now that you're investigating, he'll kill you, too."

Chapter

Thirteen

I DON'T THINK Joseph D'Angelo would stop at anything to protect himself. I mean it! He's ruthless!" John's face was flushed. "There is something cold-blooded about him. I don't trust him."

Nancy took a sip of her coffee. She remembered the first time she had heard John in the parking lot, ranting and raving at Stephanie. He was like a cannon about to go off. She was sitting across from that cannon now.

As John's voice rose, Mike Ramsey cast a few nervous glances at the other tables. A few people stared and whispered among themselves.

"Aren't you going to say anything?" John sputtered, his intense blue eyes fixed on Nancy as she sipped her coffee. "You act as if you haven't heard a word I've said. I told you this guy is dangerous!" John pounded his fist on the table so hard that the cups and silverware rattled.

A hush fell over the diner. John looked down at the table and shook his head. "I'm sorry," he said. "It's just talking about Stephanie's death . . ." His voice trailed off.

Before Nancy could reply, Mike Ramsey spoke up. "Take it easy, John," he said, but he was looking at Nancy. "This lady doesn't get scared. She's a professional."

Nancy was sure she detected a hint of sarcasm in his voice.

"Of course I get scared," she said in a level tone, looking Mike Ramsey squarely in the eye. "I'd be a fool if I didn't. I just don't let it get in the way of what I have to do."

She glanced at John Greenman. The color had drained from his face. Was he trying to throw suspicion off himself by throwing it onto Joseph D'Angelo?

Nancy reached into her bag and pulled out the letter she had found in Stephanie's room. She slid it across the table. "Did you write this?" she asked.

A look of bewilderment passed over John Greenman's face. He read the letter quickly.

"I wouldn't write these things!" he blurted out. "This isn't my handwriting." He pulled a pen from his pocket and scribbled his name on a napkin. "See for yourself."

Nancy examined the signatures on the letter and the napkin. They didn't look anything alike, but it was possible that John had been disguising his handwriting.

John seemed to sense the question in Nancy's mind. He fumbled in his pocket and brought out a piece of paper. "Take a look at this, and tell me if you think I could have written that letter."

It was a page of notes for an article. Nancy placed the napkin next to it and compared the letters in the signature with those on the page. The writing was similar. The size of the letters and the style of loops were uniform. Nancy was satisfied that the notes were made by the person who had just signed his name on the napkin.

Next, Nancy compared the notes and the signature with the letter she had found in Stephanie's room. The handwriting was completely different.

Nancy handed the notes back to John. "Any idea who would set you up?"

"No idea," John answered.

Then Mike Ramsey broke in. "John and I think the academy or the police must be covering up details of Stephanie's murder. I think a story written about the whole thing could help. It would get everything out in the open. Let the people know the truth about what's going on at this military school." He gave Nancy a hard look.

You mean a front-page byline, Nancy thought. The last thing she wanted was to have a reporter stirring things up. If he started making trouble, she might never find out who had killed Stephanie.

"Why don't you wait a little longer before putting anything in the paper, Mr. Ramsey," Nancy said evenly. "If you run an article stating your suspicions, the academy administration will panic. Then you'll get no cooperation from them."

"I was planning on making an interview with you a key part of the story," Ramsey went on.

Nancy folded her hands on the table. "If you start poking around now, you could ruin any chances of finding Stephanie's killer. Imagine this headline: Big-Shot Reporter Ruins Murder Investigation."

Mike Ramsey stood up. "Who do you think you are to tell me when I can run a story in the paper?"

John Greenman got up and stood in front of him. "She's right. Finding out who killed Stephanie is more important than a headline. You should wait."

"Think how much better a story you'll have once the killer is *caught,*" Nancy urged. "And I won't talk to anyone else. My interview with you will be an exclusive."

Mike Ramsey seemed to be thinking it over. He sat down, and a trace of his phony smile appeared on his face. "You win. I'll wait." He smoothed a hand through his hair. "But I won't wait long."

Early Monday morning Nancy hurried across campus to Cardell Hall. She hoped she'd find the academy commander in his office and that she'd be able to get him to talk to her. She knew it was a long shot, but she also knew she had to work fast. Mike Ramsey was impatient. Besides, she was supposed to be home the next day. She had an afternoon appointment back in River Heights. She had to wrap up this case, and she had to resolve the situation with Nicholas, too.

Had she really convinced herself that things between her and Nicholas would somehow work out? She wondered if her relationship with Ned would ever be the same again.

One thing at a time, she told herself. No time to worry about problems with Ned and Nicholas while Stephanie's killer is still on the loose.

Nancy entered Cardell Hall and walked down the long corridor toward the heavy mahogany door of Commander Royce's office. She held her breath and knocked.

"Who is it?" came the voice from the other side.

"Commander Royce, it's Nancy Drew. I need to speak with you."

After a moment the door opened. The commander clearly wasn't pleased to see her, but he didn't tell her to go away, either. "Come in," he said briskly. He ushered her into his wood-paneled office and motioned for her to take a seat.

"I hope your visit has nothing to do with Stephanie Grindle," he said icily.

Nancy cleared her throat. "I'm afraid it does, Commander Royce."

The commander gave her a look of disgust and started walking toward the door.

"I wish you'd listen to me," Nancy said hurriedly.

The commander hesitated, then took a seat behind his desk. His face puckered as if he'd just bitten into something sour. "A perfectly competent detective has conducted a thorough investigation. His conclusion is that her death was accidental."

"I'm afraid the detective may have overlooked a few details," Nancy said bluntly.

The commander stood up and walked around the desk. He folded his arms and stood looking down at Nancy with a pinched expression. "Young lady, this academy has a reputation to uphold. We don't need someone looking to make a name for herself by starting ridiculous rumors and stirring up bad publicity."

Nancy decided to ignore the insult. "There have been too many strange things going on," she said. "If Stephanie's death was an accident, why was a threatening note sent to Tania Allens because she talked to me about Stephanie? There was a razor blade in the envelope with the note, and Cadet Allens was hurt and frightened."

The commander was silent, but Nancy knew she had his full attention.

"Why was I threatened for asking questions about Stephanie's death?" Nancy continued. "And why was I nearly trampled by a horse?"

The commander's face suddenly took on a look of impatience.

"That accident at the parade grounds yesterday had nothing to do with Stephanie's death. And if you hadn't gone around stirring up trouble, *none* of these things would be happening! If anything like what happened to Cadet Allens happens again, I'm holding you responsible. Why did you get involved in the first place?"

"Because I can't see a crime committed and just ignore it. Frankly, I don't see how you can, either."

Commander Royce opened his mouth to say something but was interrupted by a knock at the door. His assistant stuck his head in and said, "May I see you for a moment, Commander Royce? It's important."

"Excuse me," the commander said as he left the room.

Alone in the office, Nancy listened to the ticking of the clock. After a few moments, she got up and glanced at the closed office door. Then she went behind the commander's desk and started opening drawers. Commander Royce kept his drawers very neat. Pencils, papers, and pens were lined up in rows next to message pads.

When she tried the top drawer, it was locked. Her eyes scanned the top of the desk for a tool to help her pry it open. She picked up the letter opener.

Nancy slid the gleaming blade into the space between the top of the desk and the drawer. She shoved her hand up gently on the handle. Luckily, the lock was old, simple, and not very strong. The drawer opened after a few tries. She quickly removed a checkbook and began to flip through it quickly.

Most of the stubs showed that the checks had been made out to local suppliers for things like food, furniture, and equipment. Then she stopped at one notation. A check had been made out to Detective Hugh Denman for five thousand dollars, dated only two days before.

I'll bet the check was a bribe, Nancy surmised. The commander had paid off the detective to hush up Stephanie's death.

Nancy tore out the stub and stuffed it into her back pocket. She looked up, saw the door opening, and shoved the checkbook back into the drawer. She tried to close the drawer, but it wouldn't budge.

In a panic, Nancy pushed the drawer as hard as she could. It squeaked furiously as it slid closed. But it was too late. An angry Commander Royce stood before her.

Chapter

Fourteen

I SHOULD HAVE KNOWN not to leave you alone in my office," Commander Royce said. "I saw you close that desk drawer, you little snoop!"

Nancy didn't bother to deny it. Now that she had the check stub to prove that the commander had paid off Detective Denman, she didn't care how angry the commander got.

"I want you off the Stafford Academy grounds by noon today. If I see you here after that, I will have you escorted out by a security guard. Is that clear?"

Nancy didn't reply. She walked past Commander Royce and out the door of his office. Her heart was pounding as she left the building. She had to find Nicholas and tell him what she had learned.

Nancy's secret hope was that when Nicholas

saw the check stub, he wouldn't be angry at her anymore. He would see why she'd had to do what she did.

She found him on the playing field, walking alone. Their eyes met, and Nicholas stepped toward her.

"I'm sorry we quarreled, Nancy," he said, taking her hands. "I just can't stand the idea of anything happening to you."

"I understand," Nancy said. The thought that she would have to leave him so soon made her feel tangled up inside.

"I have some news," Nicholas said. "The result of the drug test on the horse's water was negative. There was nothing poisonous put into that trough."

"Another dead end." Nancy said. Except for the check stub, she was back to square one. She wasn't any closer to solving the case, and time was running out.

"Nicholas, Commander Royce has ordered me off campus by lunchtime," she said after a moment.

"He can't do that!" Nicholas said angrily.

"Apparently he can. I went to see him this morning to talk about Stephanie's death and the investigation. I might as well have been talking to a wall." Nancy gave a little shrug. "So I did what I had to do. I found this in his desk."

Nancy dug the check stub out of the pocket of

her jeans and held it out to Nicholas. "This proves that the commander made out a check to Hugh Denman for five thousand dollars."

Nicholas turned pale. "He bribed a police officer, obviously to cover up the investigation. But why?" A look of horror came into his eyes. "Do you think the commander knew Stephanie was murdered? Is it possible he even had something to do with it?"

Nancy considered the questions for a few moments. "Those are very real possibilities. He paid the detective a lot of money, so he must have thought he had an important reason." Nancy bit her lip. "Of course, he may have thought it was important to avoid bad publicity for the school."

"Okay," Nicholas said. "I'll handle everything from here on in. We've got to get it all out in the open."

Nancy stared at him. He was trying to take over again. She couldn't let it happen.

"This is *my* investigation, Nicholas, and I still have a few hours left to find out who killed Stephanie. Until then, I don't want anything out in the open. Once the case is solved, we can go to the police with the whole story—the cover-up, the bribe, *and* the killer."

Nicholas folded his arms over his chest. "I'm not sure that your way is the best way. And when this is all over, what about us?"

Nancy looked away. "I don't know. You're used to having everything your way. We'd always be involved in a tug-of-war."

She paused for a moment and then added, "Besides, there's someone else. His name is Ned Nickerson. He's at school right now, but we've been together for a long time. I've felt so confused about everything all weekend."

"Isn't there room for someone else in your life, Nancy?"

Nancy could feel her stomach tightening into a knot. "I want to see you again, Nicholas. At the same time, I'm not sure that I should." Nancy looked into his eyes. "What about you? There must be someone special in your life, too."

Nicholas was silent for a moment. "Yes," he said. "At least, I thought so, until I met you."

"Tell me about her."

"Her name is Andrea. I met her over summer vacation two years ago. She was the first girl who made me believe in love at first sight. I haven't dated anyone else since, or even looked at another girl—until you."

"Why isn't Andrea here this weekend?"

"She's studying art in Europe this year. I didn't want her to go, but it was important to her. And if she hadn't," he added, "I wouldn't have met you."

Nancy sighed. "So we've both been feeling guilty this whole weekend. It's true, isn't it?"

"Yes." Nicholas moved closer to Nancy. "But I can't help the way I feel about you."

He was about to say more when Bess came running toward them, her cheeks red and her eyes sparkling.

"Come on, you two," she said, out of breath. "You're going to be late for the farewell party!"

Nancy took a deep breath. "I'm sorry, Bess, but I can't go. I've been asked to leave Stafford Academy by noon."

Bess's eyes widened. "Why?"

Nancy filled her in on what had happened in Commander Royce's office. "I've only got a few hours left, and I want to go through the whole case and see if I can put it all together."

"Well, George and I will help. I'll go find her and tell her we have to leave soon."

"You don't have to, Bess. You two are having such a good time. Stay and enjoy yourselves."

Bess put her hands on her hips. "No way! You know we wouldn't stay here when you've been told to leave. Besides," she added, "you're our ride. I'll go find George." She turned and trotted off.

After she was gone, Nancy and Nicholas stood in silence for a moment. When Nicholas started to speak, Nancy interrupted. "Not now,

Nicholas, please. Let's talk later." She pressed the check stub into his hand. "Hang on to this for me. If the commander discovers that it's gone, he won't suspect that you have it. I'll meet you by the main gate at noon—or whatever that is in military time. Okay?" Nancy smiled at him.

Nicholas nodded and put the check stub in his pocket.

Nancy knew that her feelings for Nicholas were strong, but deep down she knew things between them would never work the way they did between her and Ned. She never felt that Ned was trying to take over or intrude on her territory. There was a comfortable balance with Ned that she and Nicholas could never have.

As Nancy walked across campus on her way to the hotel, her eyes lingered on every detail. She wanted to remember it all—the majestic buildings and rolling hills, the trees bright with color, the smartly stepping cadets in uniform.

When she reached the hotel, Nancy's mind was clear, and she was ready to focus totally on the case. I have to wrap up this case in two hours, she thought as she turned the key in the lock.

Nancy pushed the door open. There was a manila envelope on the floor. She picked it up carefully and undid the clasp. Instead of reaching inside, she tipped the envelope to let the contents fall on the floor.

There was no razor blade, just a single sheet of white bond paper. On it was scrawled: "Get out now, or what happened to Stephanie will happen to you."

Chapter

Fifteen

NANCY HELD the note in her hand and almost shouted with excitement. The clues were coming together at last.

She got out her book and took it over to the small desk in the corner of the room, then sat down and took out the threatening note that Tania had received along with the letter she'd found in Stephanie's room. She laid the two pieces of paper alongside the note she had just found.

Nancy examined the three pieces of paper closely. One by one, she held them up to the light.

"Yes!" she said. She pulled out the scrap of paper that Tania Allens had written her room number on. It was time to have a talk with Tania right now.

"Is Cadet Allens in her room?" Nancy asked the officer at the desk when she reached Tania's barracks.

The guard, a middle-aged man whose dark hair was graying at the temples, surveyed the sign-in book. "She's here," he said. "Hasn't been out all morning."

"Thanks." Nancy brushed a strand of hair off her forehead. "I'd like to go up and see her." She flashed her guest pass, and the guard nodded.

Nancy's footsteps echoed along the tiles as she walked down the long corridor toward Tania's room. She knocked on the door and waited with anticipation.

When there was no answer, Nancy knocked louder, rapping the door hard with her knuckles. Again, no answer. She put her ear to the door. She heard nothing.

No matter what the sign-in book said, Tania wasn't in. So where was she?

As Nancy walked across the campus, she considered a list of places that Tania might be.

Would she go to the dining hall? No, breakfast was over and lunch hadn't started. The dining hall would be closed.

She'd try the stable, then the café, then the library, Nancy decided. She broke into a jog as she approached the stables. Inside, a few cadets were grooming horses. Joseph D'Angelo glared when he caught sight of Nancy.

"Have you seen Tania Allens?" she asked.

"No," D'Angelo said with a sneer. "What makes you think I'd tell you, anyway?"

Nancy ignored the dig and turned her back on D'Angelo. She didn't have time to play games with him.

"Nancy, wait!" he called.

Nancy hesitated, then turned to face him. He draped the rag he had been using over the side of the stall and rubbed his hands on the legs of his pants.

"Look, Nancy," Joseph said. "I don't care if you think I'm a hothead. You don't have to like me. But just know I'm not a killer."

"I know you didn't kill her, Joseph. I believe you," Nancy said quietly.

D'Angelo flashed her a genuine smile.

"Now I'll ask you again," Nancy said. "Have you seen Tania Allens?"

Joseph picked up the rag and shook his head. "No. Honestly, I haven't."

"Thanks," Nancy called over her shoulder as she ran from the stable. She sprinted to the boathouse café.

There were a few cadets at the tables. In one corner a couple held hands and stared into each other's eyes. Tania was nowhere to be seen.

Suddenly, Nancy got an idea. She set off at a

fast jog, heading for the trail where maneuvers were conducted. She wasn't surprised to see Tania there alone. She was down on her knees, appearing to search frantically for something. "Tania!" Nancy called.

Tania Allens whirled around. "Nancy! What are you doing here?"

"Looking for you," Nancy said quietly. She looked around. "This is where Stephanie's body was found."

"Really?" Tania gave a tight little smile that didn't quite seem real to Nancy. "It's just a spot in the woods, that's all. I like to come here. It's peaceful." Tania shivered and pulled her jacket close.

"You look chilly, Tania," Nancy said. "Why don't you put on your hat?" When Tania didn't reply, Nancy continued, "Is that what you were looking for—the hat you lost when you were struggling with Stephanie? And did you think that threatening note of yours would scare me?"

The smile on Tania's face faded. "Huh? Someone sent you a threatening note, too? It must be the same person who sent the note to me."

"You're right," Nancy said, moving in a little closer. "You ought to know, because you sent them both."

Tania froze. Nancy could see beads of perspiration on her upper lip. "What are you doing, playing a joke on me?" Her voice sounded hollow and tinny. "Did you find out who killed Stephanie?"

Nancy looked straight into Tania's eyes and nodded. "I figured it all out. You wrote the threatening notes, *and* you wrote the threatening letter signed 'John.'"

Tania took a step backward. "How did you know?"

"From the stationery. The notes you wrote all had the same watermark, a flying *A*. It was on the piece of paper you wrote your room number on, too."

"So what?" Tania's voice was high and strained. "Anyone can buy that stationery."

Tania began shifting from her left foot to her right and back again. An eager, hopeful smile appeared on her face. "Lots of people buy Allens stationery." She began talking faster and faster, the words tumbling over each other.

"I know lots of people buy Allens stationery," she continued, "because my father sells so much of it, he's rich. He's so rich and powerful that everyone is afraid of him. Everyone has to do what he says." Tania twisted a piece of her hair. "Especially me."

"Tania, Allens stationery isn't sold at the academy supply store, so the cadets don't use it. But you can get it easily because your parents own the company, and you have an endless supply."

Tania's shoulders sagged. Every ounce of energy seemed to have drained from her.

"Why did you kill Stephanie, Tania?" Nancy asked.

Tania hugged her arms over her chest. "I *had* to stay at Stafford. My dad went here, and my brother and sister both graduated with honors. I did the best I could, but from the first day, Stephanie picked me out and gave me a hard time. She was always riding me. She never let up. I knew she wouldn't stop until she got me thrown out."

Tania leaned against a tree. "I didn't mean to kill her, though."

"Then how did it happen?" Nancy asked.

"The night of the dance, I saw Stephanie from my window. She was dressed in sweats, so I figured she was going running. I hurried after her. I wanted another chance to run the course. But when I finally caught up with her, she laughed at me. She said she'd already written a report calling for my dismissal from school. She said I was a loser.

"I don't know what came over me, but suddenly I couldn't stand it anymore. I just started pushing her. I wanted to see *her* get scared for a change."

Tears began rolling down Tania's cheeks. "I pushed her down on the ground, but she got back up. I pushed her again, but this time she slipped on some leaves. She hit her head on a rock and stopped moving. I knew I had done something awful to her. I started running and running and running. The next thing I knew, I was back in my room. I realized I had lost my hat, so I went back to look for it. But then there was a huge crowd. That's when I ran into you."

Tania was sobbing now. "I knew I could get away with it if I just kept calm. My name wasn't in the hat. Plus I knew lots of cadets had seen Stephanie and her boyfriend fighting, so I wrote a threatening letter and signed his name. I brought it to Stephanie's room. I made a mess of the place finding the report she'd written about me. I took it and planted the letter I had forged. I thought of everything."

Tania stopped crying suddenly. Her usual meek expression did not return to her face. Instead, her features twisted into an angry knot.

"Stephanie exaggerated my failures. She even reported things that weren't true, like being late to drills and even missing them. I have never missed a practice. And I've always worked extra hard. She didn't want me to have a chance to succeed." Tania looked at Nancy, her eyes flashing. "When I read the report, I was glad she was dead."

"Are you still glad, Tania?"

"Why shouldn't I be?" Tania said. "She could have helped me, but she didn't. If I got thrown out, my life would be ruined, but she didn't care."

Her mouth twisted into a grim smile. "I needn't have bothered with the letter. The detective never found it. He hardly searched her room. I know, because I watched him. The academy commander didn't want to believe anything had happened to Stephanie. I heard him talking to the detective about how worried he was about bad publicity for the school. He thought it would reflect on him and he might lose his job. Everything would have been fine— if you hadn't shown up."

She looked at Nancy with wide, sad eyes.

Cautiously, Nancy took a few steps toward Tania. "We've got to get you some help," she said.

Tania eyed her warily. "What do you mean?"

Nancy kept her voice low and steady. "You killed someone, Tania."

"I didn't mean it! I didn't mean to kill her!" Tania began to shout wildly.

"I know you didn't mean to do it. You just need help, that's all. There are people who will understand that. Just tell them your story the way you told it to me."

"Do you really think so?" Tania had been so

wild a moment ago. Now, Nancy thought, she looked and sounded like a scared little girl.

Nancy nodded, keeping her eyes on Tania. She wasn't sure what to expect. Would Tania try to run away?

Tania looked at the ground. "All right. I'll confess." She took a step toward Nancy. But when she looked up, Nancy saw insane fury in her eyes.

In a lightning-quick gesture, Tania bent down and picked up a large rock. Then she ran straight for Nancy, the rock raised high over her head.

Chapter

Sixteen

NANCY BARELY HAD time to throw her arms up to shield herself when Tania's body slammed into her. The impact nearly knocked Nancy off her feet, but she held her ground and prepared herself for the next attack.

Tania whirled around and came at her again, still clutching the rock. The slight girl was suddenly full of strength and energy, fueled by fury.

As Tania flew at her, Nancy twisted to one side and shifted her weight. Tania was thrown off balance. She stumbled and let out a groan as she almost dropped the rock, then she whirled around and came after Nancy once more.

The cadet let out a bone-chilling shriek at the last minute, but Nancy didn't flinch as the sharp noise cut through the air. She turned aside at the last second and dealt Tania a heavy blow to the middle of her back.

The blow knocked the wind out of Tania. She arched her back in pain and fell to the ground. Slowly, she recovered, rising to her knees.

Nancy readied herself for another charge, but Tania crumpled. She sank back to the ground and buried her head in her hands.

Nancy waited a few moments, watching the defeated cadet. When she was sure it was safe, Nancy helped Tania to her feet. "It's over now, Tania," she said, leading the girl toward the main campus.

Heads turned as Nancy and Tania came up the walk toward the administration building. The cadet stared straight ahead, a blank, far-away look in her eyes.

"Someone please find Captain Dufont and ask him to come to Commander Royce's office," Nancy said to a passing cadet. He nodded quickly to Nancy and sprinted away.

Nancy and Tania continued, one step at a time, toward the commander's office. Inside the administration building, they met with silent, curious stares. Everyone moved out of their path.

Nancy knocked briefly, then pushed open the commander's door without waiting for an answer. Behind his mahogany desk, he jumped to his feet when he saw the two young women.

"Ms. Drew, I ordered you off this campus. Now I'm going to have you thrown off." He picked up the phone.

"I wouldn't do that if I were you, Commander," Nancy said coolly. She helped Tania into a chair. "The game is over. Nicholas Dufont and I know all about the cover-up."

The commander's body stiffened, and he hung up the phone. Then, in a split second, he regained his composure. "Don't be ridiculous," he said.

"Tania Allens is here to confess to the killing of Stephanie Grindle," Nancy said. "She's already told me the whole story."

Tania shrank back in the overstuffed chair and looked out the window. "It's true," she said in a voice barely above a whisper.

The commander's eyes widened. "That's impossible. That young woman wasn't murdered—it was an accident. It's all been investigated. Detective Denman said—"

Nancy cut him off. "Detective Denman said what you wanted him to say. I know you bribed him, Commander. Denman's career is over, and yours is, too."

Commander Royce stood still, clenching and unclenching his fists.

Nicholas, Charlie Burke, and Trevor Austin

burst into the office. "Nancy, are you all right?" Nicholas asked, hurrying toward her.

"Yes." Nancy smiled. "I'm fine."

"I came as soon as I got your message," Nicholas said. "I've called the police, and they're on their way." Nicholas shot Commander Royce a look of contempt.

"I was only thinking of the school," the commander said thinly. "The publicity—the scandal would have been the end of our endowment." He bowed his head. "I didn't think for a moment that the girl had been murdered."

"You were thinking of yourself and your own reputation. It had nothing to do with the school." Nicholas shook his head. "You've violated every military honor code and set a terrible example as a leader."

The commander remained silent. He sank into his seat and clasped his hands in front of him on his desk.

Trevor Austin was pale. "I'm sorry, Nancy. For everything. I guess I've got a lot to learn."

Nancy nodded her acceptance of his apology.

When the police arrived, Nancy told them everything she had found out, then she excused herself.

"Come outside with me for a minute," Nicholas said, following her into the hallway. He slipped Nancy's arm in his as they walked out onto the building's columned porch.

"I guess it's almost time for you to go," Nicholas said.

"Yes," Nancy said simply, looking into the deep blue-gray eyes that had drawn her to him when they'd first met. An unspoken understanding that their romance was over passed between them.

"Will I ever see you again, Nancy?" he asked her.

Nancy sighed. "I don't think I can answer that now. Maybe after some time has passed."

Nicholas gently touched her cheek with his fingertips. "I'd like that." He held her close and stroked her hair gently.

"You're an incredible person," he said softly, then let her go. They turned and went their separate ways.

Two weeks later, Nancy, Bess, and George sat in Nancy's den. "Stop hogging the popcorn, please," Bess said.

Nancy handed over the bowl. "Look at this," she said, shuffling the pages of a newspaper. "Mike Ramsey got his wish. A front-page story exposing the cover-up of the investigation into Stephanie Grindle's death."

"What does it say?" George prompted. "Give us the gory details."

"Gladly." Nancy skimmed the article. "Commander Royce was thrown out of the academy. It says here that he'll never be able to serve in the military again, and that he also had to pay a fine and perform some form of public service. An interim academy commander will take over until a new one can be found."

"What does it say about Tania Allens?" Bess asked.

Nancy scanned the page again. "There isn't much else we don't already know. Tania Allens is in a psychiatric hospital."

Nancy folded the newspaper. As Bess and George continued talking, her thoughts drifted to Ned. She hadn't seen him since she'd come back from Stafford, but they'd spoken on the phone. She had told him all about the case, and she had mentioned Nicholas but said nothing about what went on between them.

She knew she'd have to tell Ned the truth, but she didn't want to do it over the phone. She wanted to tell him in person. But Ned told her he was busy at school, and he didn't know when he could get away.

Nancy stared out the window. She knew she wouldn't feel ready to put the Stafford Academy case behind her and move on until she had gotten everything out in the open between them. Until then, Nicholas Dufont hovered between them like a gray cloud.

Out of the corner of her eye, Nancy saw a

figure coming through the doorway of the den. It was a young man, tall and broad-shouldered, with wavy brown hair. He wore a short leather jacket and blue jeans and moved with easy assurance.

"Ned," Nancy breathed. She threw down the newspaper and ran to welcome him. In a moment, he was beside her, pulling her close.

Nancy threw her arms around him, inhaling the clean scent of his skin, an aroma that was a mixture of soap, shampoo—and Ned.

Bess and George took a look at the two of them and said their goodbyes.

Nancy took Ned's hand and led him into the den. For a few minutes they sat on the sofa talking about what they had been doing the past few weeks. Nancy quickly filled Ned in on the latest details of the case.

"Nancy, I think you attract danger," Ned said when she had finished. "Now, tell me what else happened that weekend."

Nancy looked at him in surprise. He knew her so well, she thought as she took a deep breath.

"It's all in the past tense, Ned. My date, Nicholas, and I were attracted to each other, but I realized that it was all wrong. No one could be right for me the way you are."

She looked into Ned's eyes, trying to read

what he was thinking. Her heart hammered in her chest. Would their years together be lost, or would he understand?

After a moment Ned took Nancy in his arms. "Don't ever forget what you just said, Nan," he said. His lips brushed her forehead.

"I won't," she whispered, and rested her head on his chest.

The newspaper lay on the coffee table where Nancy had thrown it. On the front page was a picture of Nancy, Nicholas, Tania Allens, and a police officer. Nancy and Ned glanced at the picture at the same time.

"So, the case is wrapped up for good?" Ned asked.

Nancy looked deep into Ned's eyes. She put her arms around her boyfriend and kissed him.

"For good," she said.

Nancy's next case:

There's mystery! There's romance! There's danger! A preview of coming movie attractions? No. It's a preview of the real world Nancy's about to enter as she hops a jet to Hollywood. Famed film director James Jackson—a friend of her father—has fallen victim to a blackmailer, and Nancy's on the scene. Ten million dollars and Jackson's new movie are at stake, and so is Nancy's heart—as she and the movie's screenwriter create a few scenes of their own. But a new romance could turn into a dangerous distraction. The blackmailer has a new target—Nancy Drew—and the plan is to cut her out of the picture for good . . . in *Dangerous Loves,* Case #120 in The Nancy Drew Files™.

Now your younger brothers or sisters can take a walk down Fear Street....

R·L·STINE'S GHOSTS OF FEAR STREET®

1	Hide and Shriek	52941-2/$3.99
2	Who's Been Sleeping in My Grave?	52942-0/$3.99
3	Attack of the Aqua Apes	52943-9/$3.99
4	Nightmare in 3-D	52944-7/$3.99
5	Stay Away From the Tree House	52945-5/$3.99
6	Eye of the Fortuneteller	52946-3/$3.99
7	Fright Knight	52947-1/$3.99
8	The Ooze	52948-X/$3.99
9	Revenge of the Shadow People	52949-8/$3.99
10	The Bugman Lives	52950-1/$3.99
11	The Boy Who Ate Fear Street	00183-3/$3.99
12	Night of the Werecat	00184-1/$3.99
13	How to be a Vampire	00185-X/$3.99
14	Body Switchers from Outer Space	00186-8/$3.99
15	Fright Christmas	00187-6/$3.99
16	Don't Ever get Sick at Granny's	00188-4/$3.99
17	House of a Thousand Screams	00190-6/$3.99

A MINSTREL BOOK

Christopher Pike presents....
a frighteningly fun new series for your younger brothers and sisters!

SPOOKSVILLE

The Secret Path 53725-3/$3.50
The Howling Ghost 53726-1/$3.50
The Haunted Cave 53727-X/$3.50
Aliens in the Sky 53728-8/$3.99
The Cold People 55064-0/$3.99
The Witch's Revenge 55065-9/$3.99
The Dark Corner 55066-7/$3.99
The Little People 55067-5/$3.99
The Wishing Stone 55068-3/$3.99
The Wicked Cat 55069-1/$3.99
The Deadly Past 55072-1/$3.99
The Hidden Beast 55073-X/$3.99
The Creature in the Teacher
00261-9/$3.99
The Evil House 00262-7/$3.99

A MINSTREL BOOK